A man could take only so much temptation

The house was quiet except for the pounding of Langley's heart. He had told himself over and over the reasons he shouldn't make love to Danielle, but right now he couldn't remember one of them. He couldn't think at all, not with her mouth on his. His body was going crazy with a hunger that robbed him of control and scared him to death.

She wanted him. He wanted her, wanted her so desperately that just her kiss seared into his very soul. He couldn't understand his feelings for her. They had come on so fast and so strong, so different from anything he'd experienced before. All he knew was that he had to make love with her before they had no time left....

Dear Harlequin Intrigue Reader,

Sunscreen, a poolside lounge—and Harlequin Intrigue: the perfect recipe for great summer escapes!

This month's sizzling selection begins with *The Stranger Next Door* (#573) by Joanna Wayne, the second in her RANDOLPH FAMILY TIES miniseries. Langley Randolph is the kind of Texan who can't resist a woman in trouble. Can he help unlock a beautiful stranger's memories...before a killer catches up with her first?

Little Penny Drake is an *Innocent Witness* (#574) to a murder in this suspenseful yet tender story by Leona Karr. The child's desperate mother, Deanna, seeks the help of Dr. Steve Sherman. Can Steve unlock her daughter's secrets...and Deanna's heart?

Dr. Jonas Shades needs a woman to play his wife. Cathlynn O'Connell is the perfect candidate, but with time running out, he has no choice but to blackmail his bride. Each minute in Jonas's presence brings Cathlynn closer to understanding her enigmatic "husband" *and* closer to danger! Don't miss *Blackmailed Bride* (#575) by Sylvie Kurtz.

Bestselling Harlequin American Romance author Tina Leonard joins Harlequin Intrigue with a story of spine-tingling suspense and dramatic romance. She's created the small town of Crookseye Canyon, Texas, as the backdrop for *A Man of Honor* (#576). Cord Greer must marry his brother's woman to keep her and her unborn baby safe. But is it fear that drives Tessa Draper into Cord's arms, or is it something more than Cord had hoped for?

Indulge yourself and find out this summer—and all year long!

Sincerely,

Denise O'Sullivan
Associate Senior Editor
Harlequin Intrigue

The Stranger Next Door
Joanna Wayne

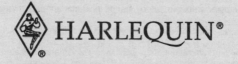

TORONTO • NEW YORK • LONDON
AMSTERDAM • PARIS • SYDNEY • HAMBURG
STOCKHOLM • ATHENS • TOKYO • MILAN • MADRID
PRAGUE • WARSAW • BUDAPEST • AUCKLAND

ISBN 0-373-22573-3

THE STRANGER NEXT DOOR

Visit us at www.eHarlequin.com

Printed in U.S.A.

ABOUT THE AUTHOR

Everyone loves a cowboy, and Joanna Wayne is no exception. Although she lives just a few miles from steamy, exciting New Orleans, she always enjoys her trips to the neighboring state of Texas. While there, she delights in becoming just one of the hands. From riding the range to rounding up cattle by helicopter, she finds plenty to keep her busy and lots of wonderful plot ideas to enhance her stories of romance and suspense. She is sure that as long as there are rugged men who love their cattle, their land and their lifestyle, there will be women who fall in love with them. The fact that the cowboys look so sexy in their boots, jeans and Stetsons is only icing on the cake. You can write to Joanna at P.O. Box 2851, Harvey, LA 70059.

Books by Joanna Wayne

HARLEQUIN INTRIGUE
288—DEEP IN THE BAYOU
339—BEHIND THE MASK
389—EXTREME HEAT
444—FAMILY TIES*
471—JODIE'S LITTLE SECRETS
495—ALL I WANT FOR CHRISTMAS
505—LONE STAR LAWMAN
537—MEMORIES AT MIDNIGHT
569—THE SECOND SON*
573—THE STRANGER NEXT DOOR*

*Randolph Family Ties

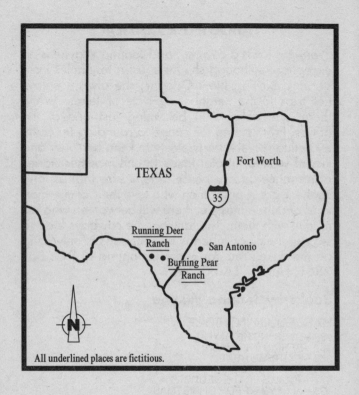

TEXAS

Fort Worth

35

Running Deer
Ranch

San Antonio

Burning Pear
Ranch

N

All underlined places are fictitious.

CAST OF CHARACTERS

Danielle — A sexy Cajun lady with a past she can't remember and a killer on her trail.

Langley Randolph — The neighboring rancher who'll do whatever he has to in order to keep Danielle safe.

Ryder Randolph — Langley's younger brother. He likes Danielle, but is afraid she will cause Langley trouble.

Milton Maccabbee — Danielle's uncle and the owner of the Running Deer Ranch, which borders the Randolph spread. He's dead but still luring Danielle into a web of danger.

Joshua Kincaid — He has his fingers in a lot of pies and they may not all be legal.

Wade Hernandez — Joshua Kincaid's ranch foreman, but he may be following his own agenda.

Samuel Drummer — He's afraid of losing his fiancé.

Corky Westmorland — Milton's stepson. He wants the Running Deer for himself.

Riff — The cantankerous old ranch hand who shows up where you least expect him.

A special thanks to Dr. Cavanaugh and his lovely wife, Donna, for always taking the time to answer my plot-related medical questions. To my grandchildren, who just by being themselves, inspire me to create adorable fictional children. And to Wayne, always.

Prologue

Danielle strolled down a side street of the famed New Orleans French Quarter. She shifted the bulk of her packages from one shoulder to the other and stretched the muscles in her neck. She was tired from the tips of her toes to the top of her head, but it was a good kind of tired. She'd spent the day sightseeing and shopping.

And, of course, eating. Sugary beignets, steaming café au lait, shrimp po-boy sandwiches. By late afternoon, when she'd finally eaten and shopped her way from Jackson Square to the far end of Royal Street, she'd ducked into an open-air café and treated herself to a rum-and-punch drink that tasted far more innocent than it felt. She was just a tad giddy now, ready for a quick shower before she collapsed in front of the TV.

By this time tomorrow, she'd be in Kelman, Texas. She'd be opening long-shut closets and rattling family skeletons that might be better left hidden away. She'd have been there today if she'd known her friend Beth was going to have to rush out of town on an unexpected family emergency. But there was no reason to change her flight plans. The day's break gave her a chance to spend time in one of her favorite cities.

She stopped at the corner to get her bearings. Her

hotel was nearby—at least she thought it was. Fishing in her pocket, she pulled out the map she'd picked up at the hotel. She unfolded it, manhandling the unwieldy square of paper until she could catch enough illumination from the streetlight.

Running her finger down the crease, she located the X that marked the location of the hotel. It was two blocks west of where she was standing and one block back toward the river. About two blocks more than she felt like walking but not far enough to justify taking a taxi.

She turned down the side street, the most direct route. It was the same street she'd taken this morning when she'd left the hotel, but it looked different at dusk. Without the warming glow of the sun, the century-old buildings were stark and intimidating. Worse, the daytime crowd had gone home and the night revelers hadn't appeared on the scene.

Actually, there was no one around except a skinny guy leaning against a balcony support post a few yards in front of her. He stared at her openly and then took the cigarette that dangled from his mouth and dropped it to the street, grinding it beneath the toe of his scuffed shoe.

The concierge's warning ran through her mind. *The Quarter is safe as long as you stay on the main streets, the ones populated with tourists.*

Apprehension quickened her pulse. She considered going back the way she had come, but the man turned and disappeared inside a doorway right behind him.

She stopped at the corner, then crossed the street. One more block to the river. A boat whistle blasted in the distance. A series of car horns blared from the direction of Canal Street and footsteps sounded behind her. She spun around just as a man's arm wrapped around her neck.

"Let go of me!" His fist pounded against her skull. She stamped her feet and tried to twist free, but the man's grip was like iron. "Who are you? What do you want?"

He hit her again, and then she saw the blade of his knife. She kicked and tried to jerk away as he aimed it toward her chest. He missed his mark, but not completely. The blood was dripping from her side, running down her skirt and legs. She stretched her neck to get a glimpse of her attacker's face. But he wore a ridiculous Mardi Gras mask. All she could see were his eyes. Cold. Angry.

Her head was spinning. Her eyes refused to focus. And still he was hitting her with his horrible fists and dragging her away. Black walls closed in around her. And she was falling. Falling…falling…

And finally there was…nothing.

Chapter One

Langley Randolph ducked out of the rain and into the front door of Gus's Corner Café. He shook the moisture from his Stetson hat and stamped the mud from his boots.

"Not a fit night out for man nor beast," Gus called from behind the counter. He wiped his hands on the white work apron that stretched over his ample paunch. "What brings you into town?"

"Work. The storm triggered the alarm at Higgins's Supermarket. I expected as much, but I had to eyeball the place and make certain it was nothing else."

"Higgins needs to shell out a little cash and update that system. His alarm goes off if the wind blows crooked. Still, I'm glad for your company. Can I get you a cup of coffee?"

"You can." Langley shed his jacket and tossed it over one of the spare hooks supplied for the purpose. "I can use the caffeine. I've got a little more work to do before I can call it a night."

"Looks like you're serious about your temporary stint as sheriff."

"Not by choice. I'll take my cud-chewing critters to trouble-causing humans any day."

"Well, you can't blame your brother for wanting a honeymoon. If I had a wife half as pretty as Lacy, I might even chuck my boots under the bed and pull on one of them flowered Hi-waiian shirts."

"Yeah, well, it would take more than a woman for me to wear that getup."

"You just haven't met the right woman yet. Everyone said Branson would never take the plunge and he was grinnin' like a mule eatin' thistles when the preacher tightened that marriage knot around his neck."

"That was Branson. This is me." Langley settled onto a bar stool at the counter.

"This is a new brand of coffee," Gus said, setting a mug of steaming brew in front of Langley. "All the big restaurants in San Antonio have switched to it. At least that's what my supplier said."

Langley tried it while Gus watched.

"How's it taste?" he asked before Langley placed the cup back on the counter.

"Like a new brand."

"I mean, do you like it?"

"It's coffee. I liked the old brand just fine."

"You're stuck in your ways, Langley Randolph. Do you know that?" Gus leaned over the table and wiped at a stain that didn't want to give up. "Just plain stuck in your ways about everything except your cows. You got to have all the latest breeding methods on your ranch, but you want everything else about your life to stay the same. That's why you don't have a wife."

"Right. So how about one of those same old cheeseburgers you make? And a side of those same old onion rings?"

Gus grinned. "Well, at least you've got good taste. I'll fix me one and join you. I doubt I'll get any more paying customers tonight in this downpour. Everybody's home propping their feet under their own table.''

"Yeah. Too bad we didn't get this rain about August when my grass was dying from the drought.''

"Well, then we wouldn't be living in south Texas, would we?''

Gus grabbed a couple of beef patties from the cooler and plopped them onto the hot grill. They spit and sputtered, and Langley's stomach reacted appropriately. He'd have preferred to be one of the folks with their feet stretched under their own table tonight, but if he had to be out, Gus was as good company as any. Actually, better than most he'd talked to today. At least Gus didn't have any complaints he wanted to report to the acting sheriff.

Three days into his new role and Langley was eager to hand the lawman's duties back to Branson. He'd never wanted to be deputized again, but he was the only available man with any kind of experience. He'd worked as deputy for almost a year right after he'd graduated from college and filled in from time to time since then.

But he had lost his taste for the work. Now he liked running the ranch, tending his cattle, researching the latest methods for producing the best beef in the most economical fashion.

But the Randolphs always stuck together, so he couldn't very well turn down his brother's request to fill in for him for two weeks while he honeymooned. Branson had his young deputy, Gordon, on the payroll, but Gordon claimed he wasn't ready to take charge just yet. That left the job of acting sheriff to Langley.

The bell over the door tinkled, and Langley stretched his neck and looked around. Gus had been wrong when he'd said no one would be out in the storm. One more person had ventured out. A stranger. Drenched, but still attractive enough to make any red-blooded male take notice. He was no exception.

She raked a handful of wet hair from her face, tucking it behind her right ear before crossing her arms over her chest. The pose successfully hid the soft mounds of her breasts that the wet T-shirt had revealed. What she couldn't hide were the tinges of purple and dark blue, remnants of bruises that covered her face and arms. Instinctively, Langley's guard went up.

The woman stepped toward the counter. "Can I help you?" Gus asked. "You surely didn't come out in this thunderstorm for a burger and fries."

"No, I'm looking for the sheriff. I was told he might be able to help me. Do you know where I could find him?"

Trouble. Langley knew it the way a man knows his horse is about to buck or that the branding iron is not quite hot enough to do the job. He didn't know how he knew it. He just did.

He slid from his stool. "I'm Langley Randolph," he said, "the county sheriff—at least I am this week. What can I do for you?"

"I hate to ask on a night like this, but I'd appreciate a lift to the Running Deer Ranch."

He studied the woman. Even soaked through to the skin, she had a sophistication about her. And an accent he didn't recognize. "Do you have business at the Running Deer?"

She nodded. "I'm Danielle, Milton Maccabbe's niece. I'm here to see him."

Langley ran his hands deep into his front pockets, debating with himself on how he should tell the dripping stranger with a strange accent that the man she was planning to visit had died two weeks ago. "I'd be happy to give you a ride, but—"

"Good," she broke in. "I'm anxious to get out there and I'm without transportation."

"Then how did you get to Kelman? We're a long walk from nowhere."

"I came by bus."

So that explained why she was soaking wet. Kelman didn't have a regular bus station, but if there was someone to pick up or let off, the bus stopped at Phil Klinger's feed store. But it was half past seven. The place would be locked up tight this time of night.

"The driver suggested I call the sheriff from the pay phone where he dropped me off, but it wasn't working. I guess the storm knocked it out. I saw the sign for the café and took a chance it would be open." She hugged her arms more tightly around her. "I didn't expect to be lucky enough to walk right into the sheriff."

"If Langley hadn't been here, I'd have given you a ride," Gus hastened to assure her. "We Texans don't leave a woman on her own if we can help it."

"I'll drive you wherever you'd like to go," Langley said. "But I'd like to eat that burger Gus is cooking before I take off in the storm again. You might like to do the same. Gus makes the best burger in south Texas."

"The best burger in *all* of Texas," Gus corrected.

The woman turned toward the sound of the sputtering meat, her eyes wide. But she shook her head and directed her gaze back at him. "I'm not hungry, but you go ahead. I'll wait and eat something at the ranch."

Of course, she expected to have dinner with her uncle. Which meant he couldn't put off the inevitable. "I hate to be the bearer of bad news," Langley said, deciding the straight approach was the best.

"What kind of bad news?"

Langley swallowed hard and wished there was a way around what he had to say. But there wasn't. "Milton Maccabbe died a couple of weeks ago."

She lowered her head and directed her gaze to the toes of her muddy tennis shoes. "I knew he was sick," she said. "I just hadn't heard that he'd died."

"In his sleep. The doctor said it was a peaceful way to go."

"I'm glad. I just wish I'd been here."

Her voice cracked on the words, but she didn't cry. For the first time in a long time, Langley wished he was more like his brothers, wished that talking to strange women came easier to him. Instead, he was standing around like an awkward schoolboy, wondering if he should say something more or offer a shoulder to cry on.

Finally, she broke the silence. "Who's staying at the ranch now to look after the cattle?"

"Joshua Kincaid's hands are taking care of the place. Milton was foreman at Kincaid's ranch before he retired and bought the Running Deer. But no one lives there. The place is deserted once the sun goes down."

"Then I'd still appreciate a ride to the ranch, if you don't mind."

"It's not the sort of place to visit at night," Langley advised.

"I won't be visiting. I'll be moving in."

Langley rocked back on his heels. His gaze lowered from her dripping hair to the wet clothes that clung to her body like a second skin and then back to her bruised face. "I'm not sure I heard you right," he said, knowing that he had but hoping he was wrong.

"If Uncle Milton is dead, then the ranch is mine. He left it to me. I have it in writing."

"Are you a rancher?"

"No, but I can learn."

"Yep," Gus interrupted, "and if you have any trouble, you can call on Langley. He lives practically in hollering range. If there's anything about cows he don't know, it hasn't been discovered yet."

She propped a foot on the boot rail of one of the stools and leaned against the counter. "It's nice to know that expert advice will be so readily available."

"I'll be glad to help out if you have questions," Langley said. "Any of the Randolphs will, but don't put any stock in Gus's claims. Every rancher around these parts has his own way of doing things, and we all think our way's best."

"Nonetheless, I appreciate the offer." Danielle looked up at Langley, her dark eyes shadowed and mysterious, her lips parted, the flesh beneath the bruises raw. "But I'm sure I'll be selling the place as soon as I can."

Something in the way she spoke and moved reminded Langley of a frightened calf. It might just be the news of her uncle's death, but he had the strange suspicion that it was something more than grief that strained her voice and haunted her ebony eyes. More like fear. After all, someone had recently branded her with the telltale signs of violence.

"You can call on me as a rancher or as a lawman," he said. "We don't cater to abuse or abusers in Kelman."

"I don't know what you're talking about."

He stepped closer and trailed a finger along the purple marks that ran the length of her arm. She trembled at his touch and then backed away. An unfamiliar sensation swept through Langley, an awareness that set his nerves on edge. A beautiful woman with dangerous secrets— one who was about to become his neighbor.

And suddenly, Langley knew exactly how it must feel to be caught standing in the middle of a stampede with no way to escape.

HER UNCLE WAS DEAD. The news hit hard, a blow that knocked the last smidgen of confidence right out of her. All her hopes had been tied up in finding the one man who might be able to give her back her life. Now those hopes had been dashed with a single sentence out of the sheriff's mouth.

Danielle slid the wet backpack down her arms, then scooted into the booth across the table from Langley Randolph. She faked a smile and hoped the rugged cowboy couldn't hear the grumbling of her stomach when the man called Gus set a plateful of crispy onion rings between them. The last meal she'd eaten had been the lumpy oatmeal and cold toast the hospital had served for breakfast yesterday. Since then, she'd made do with a couple of cartons of milk and the crackers she'd picked up when the bus had made its pit stops.

Still, the little money her teenage roommate at the hospital had lent her would disappear fast enough without wasting it on restaurant food. Especially after she'd already used half of the meager funds to buy a bus ticket, an inexpensive backpack and a few other necessities.

Her mouth watered. She turned and stared out at the storm, but it was no use. The aroma was like a magnet, pulling her gaze back to the golden-brown slices of battered onion.

Langley pushed the plate in front of her. "Have some," he insisted. "I hate to eat alone. Besides, Gus is a very sensitive man. His feelings will be hurt if you don't rave over his speciality of the house.''

''Then I guess I'll have to try them.'' She lifted one from the plate and slipped it into her mouth. She chewed it too fast, but once her stomach had food that close, it refused to hold out any longer.

A minute later, Gus placed two more plates in front of them, each holding an oversize cheeseburger with thick slices of tomato and crisp lettuce.

''I know you said you weren't hungry,'' he said, ''but I had this cooked already. It's on the house. Just eat what you want.''

So she hadn't fooled anyone. Obviously, she wasn't a good actress. She hoped that wasn't what she'd done for a living before...before she'd almost wound up dead. Before her life had slipped away in a black cloud of desperation.

She forced her mind back to the present. ''Thanks, Gus,'' she replied, her fingers already closing around the sesame-seed bun. ''If the burger is as good as the onion rings, I'll be able to eat it even if I'm not hungry.''

''Good. You eat up. Keep Langley here company, but don't let him bore you with talk about those cows of his.''

''I promise not to get bored.'' She bit into the burger as Gus walked away. Her taste buds danced deliriously. After two weeks of hospital food and two days of starvation, the thick, juicy beef was like manna from heaven.

She felt Langley's eyes on her while she ate and knew he was sizing her up, but even that wasn't enough to squelch her enjoyment of the meal. With all the problems she had, any pleasure at all was a cause for celebration.

Langley didn't say a word until she'd finished everything on her plate, but the second the last bite was swallowed, he propped his elbows on the table and leaned in close. "I'm kind of surprised to hear that Milton had a niece. I'd heard he didn't have any family."

She stared him down. "I guess you heard wrong." His attitude annoyed her. More to the point, it made her nervous. As nervous as the badge on his shirt did. She'd had enough of arrogant lawmen over the past two weeks.

They'd interrogated her endlessly and then doubted her answers. They'd poked into her affairs and then questioned her integrity.

"Were you a friend of my uncle's?" she asked, hoping to throw the focus of the conversation on something other than herself. Besides, she needed all the information she could get, and the sooner the better.

Langley leaned back in his chair. "I wouldn't say your uncle and I were friends. More like acquaintances."

"But you did know him?"

"We were neighbors. My family owns the Burning Pear Ranch, and it borders the Running Deer. We're separated by a creek that's dry about half the time and by miles of barbed wire."

"So you live by the theory that good fences make good neighbors?"

"Absolutely. Especially in cattle country."

The sheriff was smiling now, a nice open smile that curled his lips and touched his dusky gray eyes. Maybe she'd been too quick to judge. But then, she was in no position to trust anyone, especially a stranger who, like it or not, was probably going to know as much about her as she knew about herself before long.

Langley swirled the coffee in his white mug, then drank it down to the last drop before pushing the empty cup to the side. "Have you ever been to the Running Deer?"

She managed a smile, thankful the sheriff had asked one of the few questions that fitted her standard reply. "Not that I remember." She wiped her mouth with her napkin, then placed it on the table. "But I'm anxious to see it. Can we get started now?"

He met her gaze but made no move to get up. "Are you planning on spending the night there?"

"Of course." Something in his expression sent new waves of alarm careening through her senses. "There is a house, isn't there?"

"Of sorts. It's a little run-down and short on modern conveniences."

"I'm sure I'll manage."

"As long as you don't mind roughing it."

Langley reached into his back pocket and pulled out a few bills. He tucked them under his plate, then finally stood, moving in a slow, languid manner that was strangely seductive. Or maybe it was the bronzed flesh beneath the sun-bleached hair or the rugged cast to his youthful face that generated the masculine appeal.

"I'll drop you off and stay while you check out the condition of the place," he proposed. "If you change your mind about wanting to stay out there, I'll run you back into town to the motel."

"I'm tough. I can handle a few nights without luxuries." At least she hoped she was tough. If she wasn't, life was about to become even more unpleasant than it already had been in the past couple of weeks. Because like it or not, the Running Deer was now home. The only one she had.

She joined Langley in saying goodbye to Gus and offered a genuine thank-you for her food, assuring him it was the best she'd eaten in a long time. It was nice to be totally honest for a change.

Langley held out his jacket and then slipped it over her shoulders when she accepted. The early November wind was cutting, but the downpour had slowed to a drizzle by the time they left the café and walked the few steps to Langley's pickup truck. He opened the door and she climbed inside. She waited for the chills of apprehension to close around her heart as Langley slid behind the wheel and slammed his own door shut.

But for the first time in two weeks, her pulse didn't race and her stomach didn't tie itself into ratty knots at the prospect of being alone with a strange man. Maybe her psychological scars were starting to heal the way her physical ones had. Or maybe a stalwart cowboy lawman in a small Texas town far away from New Orleans didn't unnerve her the way every man who'd entered her hospital room had.

Now all she had to worry about was what she was going to do on a ranch when all she knew about cows was that they gave milk or became steak. And all she knew about herself were the images that haunted her mind, like a video that played the same terrifying scene over and over again.

She shivered, suddenly all too aware that she was about to be alone on a ranch in the middle of nowhere with only the ever-running tape in her mind for company. It wouldn't take long to find out just how tough she really was.

LANGLEY TURNED IN AT the Running Deer Ranch, surprised to find the gate unlatched and swung open. He got out of the truck and closed it behind them, suspicion running rampant in his usually trusting mind. Maybe it was the badge that had changed him, or maybe it was just that in trying to fill Branson's shoes, he had adopted the same doubting-Thomas nature that had always ruled his older brother.

At any rate, the open gate wasn't the only thing troubling him. He had serious doubts that the woman sitting beside him had told him the whole truth. She'd come by bus to claim a ranch she'd said her uncle had left her, only she didn't even know the man had died. Her declared intentions were to stay at the ranch, but the only thing she carried that resembled luggage was the soaking wet backpack.

She'd also claimed she wasn't hungry back at Gus's, but he'd never seen a woman eat quite that fast or appear to enjoy her meal more. And she was nervous, constantly rubbing the back of her neck or wringing her hands. When she caught him looking at her, she'd stop and sit straight, staring out into the darkness.

He'd do some investigating in the morning, find out if the Running Deer had been turned over to her. Of course, first he'd have to find out her last name. She'd been stingy even in that department, changing the subject when he'd asked.

A few minutes later, he pulled to a stop in front of the cabin. It looked even worse in the dark than it did in the daylight, if that was possible. Most of the shutters were missing, part of the railing was off the narrow porch, and the edge of the bottom step had rotted away.

"This is it," Langley said, turning the truck so that his headlights illuminated the front door. He adjusted the delay on the lights so they'd stay on until Danielle had time to maneuver the dilapidated stairs.

She stared at the cabin. "Milton lived here?"

"He did. Right up until the day he died. But then,

your uncle didn't seem to require much in the way of creature comforts. He liked to fish and he liked to raise cattle. Actually, the ranch buildings are in much better shape than his cabin.''

"That's Uncle Milty for you.''

But in spite of her flippant reply, her step was hesitant as she climbed down from the truck. Langley studied her profile, the bruises on her cheeks and chin taking on an almost ghoulish appearance in the glow of the headlight beams.

He walked over and took her elbow, half-expecting her to pull away. She didn't. Instead, she took a deep breath and exhaled slowly.

"Looks like I'm home,'' she said. ''I appreciate your giving me a lift out here, but you don't need to stay. I'm sure you have work to do.''

"I'll go in with you and have a look around, make sure no wild animals have taken over the place since it's been vacated.''

She whirled around. "What kind of wild animals?''

"I don't know. Polecats. Coyotes. Rats.''

"You're joking, right?''

A coyote bayed in the distance as if in answer to her question. She shuddered.

"Do you still want me to leave you on your own?'' he asked.

She shook her head, and her hair tumbled over her face. Tangled and disheveled, it was beginning to dry, falling waywardly about her cheeks and giving her the appearance of an impish nymph.

She fished a brass key from the pocket of her jeans. "This should open the door.''

"I doubt it's locked. You don't get a lot of uninvited guests this far off the main road.''

He led her up the steps and turned the knob on the front door. It squeaked open as he expected. The expectations ended there, dissolved by the acid that gnawed at his stomach. A string of curses flew from his mouth as he assessed the damage.

The upholstery on the couch and an ancient recliner had been ripped to shreds, the stuffing scattered over the floor like clumps of yellow snow.

"I guess I spoke too soon," Langley said, walking to the center of the room and turning slowly so that he could better digest the sick destruction. "But I doubt whoever vandalized this place would have been deterred by a lock on the door."

Danielle took a deep breath and then walked past him.

He followed her into the kitchen and to more chaos. If a twister had picked up the house and turned it upside down, it probably wouldn't have wreaked any worse havoc. The floor and counter were littered with broken glass and scattered pans and utensils, and a steady stream of ants marched through trails of sugar and streaks of syrup that painted the floor.

Bits of glass cracked and skidded under Langley's boots as he circled the kitchen. They'd had vandals strike in Kelman before. Paint sprayed on the water tower, four-letter words carved in inappropriate places, fences cut.

But he couldn't remember hearing about anything like this, and the sight of it ground in his gut the same way the glass cut and scratched into the linoleum beneath the thick soles of his boots.

He looked up as Danielle returned from a peek at the bedroom, her face ashen, her eyes wide. He laid a hand on her shaking shoulders. "I'm sorry you had to see this. I don't know who's behind it, but right now I'm having

a hard time believing this was a group of kids out looking for excitement.''

She looked up at him, her large dark eyes haunted
pools of fear. ''No, this was done by someone who
doesn't want me here.''

''I'm sure this isn't personal.''

''Take a look in the bedroom.'' Her voice was hollow
but steady.

Langley walked to the bedroom door. The mattress
had been torn off the bed and ripped to shreds. The doors
of a small wooden chest hung open, their contents scattered about the floor. And red paint dripped from a
cracked mirror that hung over an unpainted dresser. The
letters were distorted, but the message was clear.

Get out, Danielle, or die!

Langley strode back into the kitchen and stopped in
front of the mystery guest. ''I don't want any games or
double-talk. I'd like to know what the hell is going on.
If you have a clue, and something tells me you do, now's
a good time to start talking.''

She unzipped the backpack, pulled out a folded piece
of smudged paper and handed it to him without a word.
He unfolded the letter and read it.

Danielle,

My days are numbered. The cancer is growing fast.
The doctors want me to take a lot of pills and treat-
ments, but I'm not doing it. I've lived my way. I'll
die my way.

I've made a career of making poor decisions. But
my only real regret is that I never got to know Colette's daughter. You are my only living relative,
and I'm leaving Running Deer Ranch solely to you.
I hope you choose to live on the ranch, but that

decision will be yours. You may find Kelman boring after the life you've led.

Your uncle,
Milton Maccabbe

P.S. I'm enclosing the key. You know what to do with it. I'm sorry to draw you into this, but I see no other way.

Langley folded the letter and handed it back to her. "Exactly what was it that he hated to draw you into other than this vicious destruction?"

She rubbed the back of her neck, burying her long fingers in the tangle of thick black hair. "I don't know." He started to question her response, but she held her hand up to stop him. "Don't look at me like that. I'm not lying. I just don't know."

Only he was sure she knew more than she was saying, and whatever it might be was scaring her half to death. He could read the fear in her eyes. "Let's get out of here." He touched a hand to the small of her back. "This is no place to talk."

"*You* can get out of here. I have no money and no place to go."

Her voice broke on the words, and Langley's protective side surfaced in a suffocating wave. He should maintain a professional distance from Danielle, but he wasn't Branson and he wasn't a sheriff. He was just a man who couldn't bear to see a desperate woman fighting back tears.

He reached for her hands. They were as cold as ice. "You can come home with me for the night," he said.

"You don't know me. Why would you offer to take me home with you?"

He sensed the suspicion that seemed to shadow everything she said and did. "I have no ulterior motives if that's what you're thinking. My family will be there. You'll be perfectly safe."

"So if I go with you for the night, you won't expect anything from me?"

"I didn't say that."

Anger flared in her dark eyes. "Then leave."

"I don't think so, Danielle. What I'll expect from you is plain talk. We can do it here or at the Burning Pear, but I want answers. If you're involved in something, you may as well tell me. I'll find out anyway."

"Good. Then you'll accomplish more than the police have done so far." She backed away from him. "I don't know why I should trust you, Langley Randolph, but right now, I don't have a lot of choices."

"Does that mean you're going to tell me the whole truth?"

"Yes, but let me warn you, it sounds like something straight out of a mystery novel. And if you look at me even once as if I'm lying or nuts, I'm through explaining. I've had far too many of those looks over the past two weeks."

"You've got yourself a deal. Start talking."

Chapter Two

Danielle struggled for words to describe the void she lived in. Empty rooms. Frames without pictures. A book without a cover to bind it together. A life without a past. How could she expect Langley to understand? *She* couldn't even comprehend the loss and she was forced to deal with it every second of the day.

But she might as well come clean with the whole truth. It would do no good to try to hide her vulnerability from a man who carried a badge. He'd make a few phone calls and find out the full story anyway.

Besides, if the man who'd attacked her in New Orleans had followed her to this dilapidated ranch house, if he'd been the man to create this havoc, she'd need all the help she could get.

Stuffing her hands into the pockets of her damp jeans, she sucked in a deep breath and met Langley's gaze. ''Two weeks ago, thirteen days to be exact, I was in the French Quarter in New Orleans. For some reason, I had left the beaten path and ended up on a nearly deserted street at dusk.''

''Do you live in New Orleans?''

''I don't know. Just hear me out and then you can ask questions, though I doubt I'll be able to answer them.

Anyway, I was on a side street when someone dragged me into the doorway of a building and attacked me with his fists and with a knife.''

She felt the burn of Langley's scrutiny. He was probably studying the patterns of bruises that still colored her flesh, though not nearly as vividly as they had at first. His gaze made her uneasy and she turned to face the window and stare into endless darkness.

''One of the residents of the building came downstairs and found me. He took me for dead but thankfully dialed 911. It was touch-and-go for a while, mostly due to the severity of the beating. Apparently, I'd jerked away as the man had stabbed me. The blade of the knife had veered off at an angle without damaging any internal organs.''

''Was the man who attacked you someone you knew?''

''I'm not sure.''

His mouth twisted in a scowl. ''Can you identify the perpetrator?''

''No.''

''But you must have some idea what he looked like. Was he tall, short, dark?''

''I have no memory of him, Langley. *None.* All I know of him are his eyes. I see them in my nightmares. Cold and angry.'' The words stuck in her throat, but she forced herself to continue, to say what she had to and get this over with. ''I have no memory of anything beyond the attack. My past life has virtually disappeared in a thick fog of nothingness. I don't know if I have a family. A husband? Children? A career? I don't know who I am or where I belong.''

She hated saying the words. It was as if they deleted who she was, what she might have been. Now she was a crime statistic, one reported on the back pages of the *Times-Picayune*.

Her life had been shattered, the remnants of it left in pieces so tiny she couldn't begin to put them back together again.

"A total memory loss. Amnesia."

Langley rolled the words off his tongue as if he were having trouble absorbing their meaning. But, to his credit, he wasn't looking at her like some sideshow freak, the way a couple of the hospital orderlies had. And he hadn't reverted to that I-know-you're-lying expression the New Orleans police had been so quick to adopt.

"What kind of time line did the doctors give you for the return of your memory?"

"A day, a week, a year."

"But they didn't say it was irreversible?"

"No. The neurologist said that the trauma to my system caused by repeated blows to my head and extensive blood loss was to blame and that my memory could return at any time. But according to Dr. Silvers, the staff psychiatrist, I am likely *choosing* not to face the terror of the brutal battery."

"He thinks you're blocking out the whole attack. That makes sense."

The words destroyed one more fragment of the confidence she tried so hard to maintain. "I'm glad it does to you and to Dr. Silvers because it makes no sense at all to me. What I *choose* is to know who I am and why someone tried to kill me."

"Probably some guy on drugs, desperate for cash. You just happened along at the wrong time."

Danielle leaned against the counter, clutching the edge for support. She had started shaking again, a much too common occurrence over the past two weeks. "That wasn't the investigating detective's opinion. He thinks the man might have been someone I knew. Perhaps a jilted lover or an estranged husband."

"Did he have any evidence to back up his theory?"

"Nothing concrete. He believes the severity of the attack indicates that it was personal rather than just a random robbery." She swallowed hard, her throat and chest drawing tight. "I woke up in the hospital with no clue as to who I was or how I got there."

"You must have had the letter you showed me."

"Not until two nights ago. One of the nurses stopped in and tossed an envelope onto my bedside table. She said someone from the crime lab where they were examining my bloodstained clothes had dropped it off."

"Odd that the police didn't find the letter before they sent your clothes to the lab."

"Apparently, the letter and key were stuffed into a hidden pocket inside my jacket, one neither the police nor the attacker noticed."

"Did you show the letter to the police?"

"No. I'd had enough of bureaucracy and red tape by then. And too few results. I decided to regain some control over my life and thought my uncle would be able to provide the information I needed to start doing that."

"So you simply walked out of the hospital?"

"Yes, and fortunately, the other patient in the room was a streetwise teenager who thought my story was fascinating. She's the one who lent me enough money to buy a few necessities and a one-way bus ticket to Kelman."

"How did you get your clothes back from the crime lab?"

"I didn't. One of the nurses had some things she'd

outgrown. Once I was strong enough to get around, she brought me these jeans and a couple of T-shirts. I was glad to get them. I was not about to parade through the hospital in the open-air gown they'd provided.''

She looked down at her T-shirt and noticed for the first time the way her nipples were outlined against the damp fabric. She crossed her arms over her breasts and felt an uncomfortable burn in her cheeks.

"So, now that you know as much about me as I know about myself, do you still want to take me home with you, Langley Randolph? Are you the kind of fearless man who takes chances, who thrives on being a hero?''

He nudged a loose-fitting brown Stetson back on his head. "I'm nobody's hero, Danielle. For the record, I'm a rancher who's just standing in as sheriff while my brother Branson is on his honeymoon. You can stay at the Burning Pear or not—your choice. If you decide to, you'll be welcome and safe.''

"In that case, I accept your offer of a bed. For one night. Tomorrow I'll come back over here and clean up this mess.''

"Fine, but not until after I've had the deputy dust for fingerprints.'' He reached down and picked up a piece of jagged glass. Turning, he laid it on the counter, then let his gaze lock with hers. "You don't have to clean up the cabin, you know. You can just take the advice scribbled on the mirror.''

"Leave? And go where? The trouble has already followed me from New Orleans to Kelman.'' She stepped over an inverted pot. "Right now, the ranch is the only tie I have to my past. I'm staying.'' She looked around the room again and grimaced. "Only not tonight.''

"Good. But let me warn you. My brother Ryder's never met a pretty woman he didn't take to.'' He led her through the wreckage and out the front door. "And my mom will badger you with questions. Feel free to tell her as much or as little as you like."

"I have no secrets. If I do, I don't remember them." She followed him down the steps. "How many brothers do you have?"

"There's four of us. Dillon, my oldest brother, is a Texas senator. He and his wife, Ashley, and their son, Petey, live in their own house on the Burning Pear when he's not in Austin. Branson is the honeymooning sheriff. His wife's name is Lacy. And then there's Ryder and me."

"You mentioned your mom. What about your dad?"

"He died when I was just a boy. But he was quite a man. Mom reminds us of that often enough when she's telling us what she expects of us."

"Your family sounds a little daunting."

"Us?" Langley opened the passenger-side door and held it while she climbed inside the truck. "We're just your basic cowboys."

Danielle knew nothing about cowboys, but she'd bet her last $26.92 that Langley was a cut above basic. Her spirits lifted as soon as the truck engine roared to life. A bed at the Burning Pear had to beat sleeping at the Running Deer. Tomorrow would be soon enough to set up camp in the house of horrors.

DANIELLE WOKE TO THE SOUND of laughter and a blinding stream of sunlight that poured through the window beside her bed. Pushing up on her elbows, she struggled to come to grips with morning.

Conversation wafted down the hall and under her closed door, but she could only catch an occasional word or phrase. She recognized Langley's voice, though, and the deep baritone had a soothing effect, the same way the cool freshness of the sheets had last night when she'd collapsed onto the guest bed.

She'd been spared meeting the rest of the Randolph clan last night. Langley's mother had already gone to bed and Ryder had been out. She'd been thankful. Meeting new people while disguised as a drowned rat was not her idea of fun. Come to think of it, she wondered what her idea of fun was. Whatever it was, she hadn't had any for the past two weeks.

She stretched and yawned, wincing as her body reminded her just what it had gone through at the hands of a maniac. But every day she grew stronger. Stronger and more frustrated that she couldn't find the key to unlock her memories and go on with her life.

She swung her legs over the side of the bed, shoved her feet into her shoes and walked over to stand in front of the oval cheval glass. She squinted in the sunlight, leaning close to the mirror to get a better look at the dark circles around her eyes and the hideous coloration of the healing cuts and bruises.

But at least she'd showered and shampooed her hair last night in the homey Randolph guest bath, standing under the hot spray until the tension had finally crept from her muscles and fatigue had settled in. And then she'd slicked her body with a fragrant lotion she'd found in a basket next to the stack of fluffy towels.

Now her hair fell loose and wild about her shoulders. Grabbing handfuls of it from the nape of her neck, she made a ball of the thick locks and pinned it to the top of her head with a gold-colored enamel clip, another gift from her friendly hospital mate. The only thing missing was some clean clothing to crawl into.

But she didn't have any and she couldn't very well

go strolling into the Randolph kitchen in her undies. Thankfully, she had purchased extra panties. They were cheap but served the purpose.

Funny, she could have sworn she'd left her jeans and T-shirt draped over the chair last night. But there they were, folded neatly. She picked up the shirt, ready to slide it over her head. It smelled of lemon. And it was clean.

Talk about service. But surely Langley hadn't slipped into her room while she was sleeping to collect and wash her dirty laundry. But someone had, unless the Burning Pear had good fairies on the staff.

Groaning, she forced her legs back into the stiff denim of the jeans, then tugged them over her hips. By the time she had the shirt on, she got her first whiff of brewing coffee and quickly lost interest in her appearance. She stepped into the hall and followed her nose to the kitchen.

"Open up, Betsy. It's bananas. You like bananas."

Danielle came to a quick stop in the kitchen doorway. Langley was sitting next to a high chair, shoving a tiny spoonful of mushy yellow food into the mouth of an adorable baby. It made a heart-stopping picture, but an uneasy feeling gripped her. She hadn't been prepared for seeing him in the role of daddy.

He turned and saw her, and his face split in a wide grin. "Good morning. I started to wake you for breakfast but figured you needed the sleep. Besides, Mom saved you some pancake batter. It won't take but a minute to heat up the griddle."

Langley tried to shovel another spoonful of baby food into an open mouth. This time, his young charge swung her hands, catching the end of the spoon and sending food flying onto the tray of the high chair.

"Does that mean you're full, Miss Betsy, or just that you don't want me paying attention to anyone but you?" The baby smiled and cooed, and the big, rugged cowboy playfully chucked her under her fat little chin before he wiped up the spilled food. By that time, he had sticky fingers to clean, as well. "Don't let Mom see this mess, young lady, or she'll have me bathing you before I can get out of here."

Danielle drifted toward the coffeepot. "Mom. Is that Mom as in your wife and the mother of your daughter, or Mom as in the woman who gave birth to you?"

Langley looked up from his feeding chores. "Betsy isn't *my* daughter."

"Oh. I'm sorry. I guess I jumped to conclusions. You look so right feeding her."

"I've had lots of practice. That's what happens in these equal-opportunity families." He poked the spoon back into the jar and dug around, getting the last bit of food from the bottom.

But Betsy was through eating and ready for play. She opened her mouth for the food and then let it slide out the corner of her mouth and down her chin while her eyes danced mischievously.

"In this case, practice does not make perfect," Langley admitted.

But the baby girl clearly had the cowboy just where she wanted him, wrapped tightly around her chubby little finger.

"Help yourself to coffee," Langley said. "Mom put sugar and cream out in case you wanted it. We're all straight black around here." He bent to retrieve the toy Betsy had just flung to the floor. "And, by the way, Mom is my mom. I'm not married."

Danielle felt a flicker of relief as she poured the hot

coffee into the pottery mug that apparently had been set out for her. She wasn't sure why. She certainly had no designs on the man herself. For all she knew, she was married and might even have a baby of her own.

She carried the mug back to the table and took a chair across from Langley. "So where does Betsy fit into the Randolph family?"

"Officially, she isn't kin. Unofficially, she's in the dead center of everything that goes on at the Burning Pear. For someone so little, she demands, and gets, a lot of attention."

"I can see that. She's a little heart stealer." Betsy slapped her hands against the tray, then laughed at her own antics.

Langley took the damp cloth and wiped up another smear of baby food. "We don't know who Betsy's real parents are," he continued, turning back to Danielle. "She was brought to us six months ago when she was just a newborn. The woman who delivered her to us believed Betsy was a Randolph. But, as best we can figure, the man who'd told her that had been lying. He was actually scheming to bilk us out of money."

"Had he kidnapped her?"

"We thought so at first, but the man was killed before we could find out the whole story. At any rate, we've never been able to locate Betsy's real family, so she's kind of in our care until we do."

"A mystery baby. One with a secret past. I can identify with that."

Langley nodded. "I guess you can. But there's got to be a way to check *your* past. I made some calls this morning."

The statement didn't surprise her. "Whom did you call?"

"Charity Hospital in New Orleans. The New Orleans Police Department. The detective who was handling your case."

"And what did you discover?"

"The hospital staff is very upset that you walked out without being officially released. And surprisingly enough, I learned the New Orleans cops covered all the bases, checked all the available sources for finding out who you really are. They even checked all the hotels. None of their guests were missing. And there's been no one who matches your description reported as missing either in Louisiana or anywhere across the country."

"So, it's just as I told you last night. Until my memory returns or someone reports me as missing, I'm merely an unidentified victim of a crime, fortunately a live victim."

"The problem is that without a last name or a social security number, there's nothing to hang a search on. It's just too bad Milton isn't still alive to fill in the details of your past."

"I know. I was counting on that. I tried phoning him from the hospital the night the nurse brought me the letter, but the phone company reported that the number had been disconnected."

"Even when your uncle was alive, his number was unlisted. He was not big on socializing. We can call the phone company this morning and have the phone reconnected. You'll need it if you spend any time at all over there."

She toyed with her cup, watching the brew swirl, a motion as useless as her coming to Kelman had been. Her uncle was dead. Her past was still floating in some nebulous vacuum.

Langley picked up on her mood shift. "Just because

the NOPD hasn't been able to learn your identity doesn't mean I'm giving up.''

She met his gaze. ''I'll hold you to that. You said my uncle wasn't sociable, but he must have had some friends. Maybe he told them about me.''

Langley's expression grew grim. ''I've also been on the phone with Joshua Kincaid this morning. He's the man Milton worked for before he bought the ranch and retired. Actually, it turns out Kincaid gave him the ranch, a bonus for Milton's loyalty and hard work. At least, that's the way Kincaid put it.''

''So the Running Deer was originally part of Mr. Kincaid's ranch?''

''Not part of his main ranch, but Kincaid has several land holdings in the area. He's always around to help his neighbors when they're in financial straits. He relieves them of their land at a favorable price—favorable to him.''

''But he must be charitable with his employees. He apparently was with Milton. A ranch is a generous bonus. Was Mr. Kincaid aware that my uncle planned to will the Running Deer to me?''

Langley pushed back from the table and stretched his long legs out in front of him. ''Kincaid had never heard Milton mention you. In fact, he said Milton had bragged when he first went to work for him that he was one of the world's few total loners. No family. No ties.''

The all-too-familiar sinking sensation settled in Danielle's stomach. She'd followed the one lead she had, traveled all the way to south Texas only to reach another dead end.

''Actually, Kincaid was surprised to hear that someone was claiming ownership of the Running Deer,'' Langley continued. ''He's had his men taking care of the cattle while he waited to see what was going to happen, but he said he figured the place might go on the auction block. Which is likely the real reason he's made sure the place was kept up. He's probably interested in reacquiring it.''

''But surely my uncle left a will,'' she said, grasping at straws.

''I have a man checking into that now, but don't count on it. Like I said earlier, Milton Maccabbe was a loner. He didn't socialize with any of the townspeople, didn't even have a local bank account. Lots of people speculated that he was one of those eccentric misers who had a fortune hidden in his mattress, but there's been no evidence to back that up.''

''Then that might explain the place's being wrecked. Someone was probably looking for his hidden fortune.''

''I might buy that theory if we hadn't found that warning on the mirror.''

''But it could be tied together.'' She spread her hands on the table. ''If someone knows that Milton left the ranch to me, he could be trying to make sure I don't take over before he has time to search for the millions.''

''Say, who's supposed to be the cop here?''

''It is possible. You have to admit that.''

''Right now, I have to believe anything's possible, but if some crackpot expects to find millions lying around the ranch, I think they're in for a big disappointment. According to Joshua Kincaid, Milton sank everything he had into the Running Deer. The ranch itself was as run-down as the house when he moved onto the place. He fixed all the fences and windmills, bought new equipment and invested thousands of dollars in premium breeding stock.''

"All that when he knew he was about to die? That doesn't make sense."

"It does to a cowboy. He gets his kicks riding in wide open spaces. Knows his life is worthwhile when he nurses aching muscles at the end of the day as he watches the sun set over a well-run ranch."

"Spoken like a true cowboy."

"And proud of it."

He smiled, a reaction that lit up his eyes and relaxed the muscles in his rugged face. A welcome warmth crept inside Danielle's heart. The trip to Texas hadn't lifted the thick fog of confusion concerning her past, but it had hooked her up with Langley Randolph. At the moment, that seemed a much better omen than anything that had happened in the past two weeks.

She just had to be careful not to grow too dependent on him. And not to let him become attached to her. Her life was already rife with complications, and she didn't need any more. She filed those words of caution to the back of her mind as footsteps sounded in the hall.

"I don't know how in the world a family no bigger than this one can create such a stack of—oh, I'm sorry. I didn't know our guest had joined us. She doesn't want to hear about our dirty laundry."

The smiling woman strode toward Danielle, wiping her hands on the embroidered apron that circled her plump waist. Her eyes were friendly and bright, her graying hair still shiny.

"So that explains the clean clothes. You really shouldn't have."

"Land sakes, girl, one more pair of jeans and a shirt didn't even make a showing in this pile of laundry."

"Mom, meet Danielle. Danielle, this is Mary Randolph, better known around here as Mom." Langley did the introductions as he helped Betsy out of her high chair. Betsy wrapped her arms around his neck for a quick hug and then wiggled until he put her on the floor to play with the toys she'd hurled from the high chair.

"It's a pleasure to meet you," Danielle said, extending her hand. "Your hospitality is overwhelming. And you have an extremely helpful son."

"Thank you." Mary looked at Langley and beamed. "All my boys are pretty special even if I do say so myself. Ornery at times, but special."

Langley put an arm around his mother's shoulders. "We have to be special. If we aren't, she takes us behind the woodshed and gives us what for."

"You're not too big for paddling, young man. You just think you are." She gave him a playful pat on the backside, then turned her attention back to Danielle. "I'm sure sorry I wasn't up to welcome you to the Burning Pear last night. I've been going to bed when Betsy does these days so I can keep up with her." She walked over and lifted the coffeepot as if to assure herself it wasn't empty. "Langley told me what the two of you ran into at the Running Deer. That must have been quite a shock for you, especially on top of everything else you've been through."

So Langley had told his mother everything. That was just as well. It would spare Danielle the pain of relating the sordid details all over again.

"It was a shock," Danielle admitted, "but don't feel bad about not being awake. Langley was the perfect host. I really appreciate your sharing your home."

"That's what neighbors are for. And you must be starved. I hope you like pancakes. I saved some batter. And there's plenty of bacon. I can fry you up some in no time. Or I can scramble you some eggs if you'd rather.''

''I love pancakes, but I can't let you cook for me, not after you've done my laundry.''

''Nonsense. You can't go tackling that mess at the Running Deer on an empty stomach.''

''Give up easy,'' Langley said, walking toward the door. ''No one ever wins an argument with Mom.'' He grabbed his Stetson from the shelf by the door and plopped it on his head. ''I'm going out to find Ryder. He's agreed to drive you into town for supplies, then help you clean up the mess at the Running Deer.''

''That won't be necessary.''

''No, but I like the idea of my baby brother toiling at cleanup detail. Besides, he's dying to meet you. He'll pester you anyway. You might as well get some work out of him.''

Langley left without waiting for her to comment. A few minutes later, the kitchen was filled with the mouth-watering smells of bacon frying on a cast-iron griddle. Mary cooked, moving about her roomy kitchen effortlessly, talking and smiling, with a manner that made Danielle feel as if they were old friends.

Betsy started to fuss, and Danielle picked her up, settling her in her lap. Betsy wiggled around to face her, then poked her pudgy fingers in Danielle's face. She touched Danielle's nose and grabbed for a handful of hair, pulling her topknot loose.

Gently, Danielle unwound the tiny fingers from her thick locks. So precious. Somebody's baby who'd just landed on the Randolphs' doorstep. A nice place to land, but she'd like to hear the rest of that story. She was sure Langley had omitted some interesting details.

She hugged Betsy to her chest. Somewhere she might

have a baby like this. She might have a husband, a full life that had slipped through her fingers. She might have been happy.

Or maybe not. She might have been living with the madman who'd attacked her and left her for dead.

But she wouldn't think about that now. She couldn't. She needed her strength and determination to keep functioning until her memory returned. If the letter was accurate, and if she was the Danielle it had been written to, she was the new owner of the Running Deer.

She guessed that made her a rancher. She already had the aching muscles Langley had talked about. But dealing with cows, or worse yet, a bull, was out of the question. Even a woman without a memory had to set some limits.

DANIELLE FOLLOWED the sexy young cowboy down an aisle of Higgins's Supermarket. "Ryder, you have to stop putting things in this grocery basket. I have *no* money."

"Sure you do. It's just all tied up in cows. When you manage to get the title to Running Deer free and clear, you'll sell off some of the steers and pay your debts."

"I don't think the clerk at the register will buy into that."

"Actually, she probably would if you talked to Higgins. Lots of folks around here run a credit line. But don't worry. I'm taking care of this. You can pay me back when you're solvent." He flashed a seductive smile. "In cash or favors."

"It's a good thing Langley warned me about you."

"Whatever he told you, don't believe it."

"Are you suggesting Langley would lie?"

Ryder bent to grab a giant-size bottle of bleach from

the bottom shelf. He stuffed it onto the low-riding wire shelf beneath the basket. "All joking aside, Langley is probably the most honest, unassuming Randolph of all of us. I doubt if he even knows how to flirt." Ryder grinned. "Maybe you could teach him."

"I don't know if I know how."

"My guess is you do."

"I'm not sure if that's a compliment or not."

"It's a compliment. You have that fire in your eyes, the kind of spark that goes with passion. I've seen it before. It's not something you forget."

Ryder pushed the basket to the side so that a young woman could pass. She spoke to Ryder and flashed him a wide smile. The look she gave Danielle was less than friendly.

"That lady certainly had a gleam in her eye for you. Was that the fire you were talking about?"

"No way. That was Carrie. Her dad owns a ranch just north of town. She's a sweet girl, but not my type."

"What is your type?"

"Smart. Fun. Loving. Passionate."

"And have you ever met a woman like that?"

"Once. I wasn't *her* type."

In spite of Ryder's teasing tone, she picked up a touch of bitterness. Evidently, even gorgeous cowboys sometimes had woman trouble. "Tell me, Ryder, does Langley have a significant other in his life?"

A stupid question. Before it was out of her mouth, she was sorry she'd asked it. She didn't want either Ryder or Langley to get the wrong idea. She definitely wasn't shopping for a man. For all she knew, she might have one already.

"Does Langley have a significant other in his life?" Ryder repeated the question, nodding his head and screwing up his mouth as if he were deep in thought. "Yeah. I'd have to say he does. A bunch of them. They all have four legs and hooves."

Ryder was teasing again, and his easy humor made the awkwardness of the moment disappear. She liked his way. It made her feel normal, let her almost forget that she was the only one walking around the grocery store who didn't have a clue as to who she really was.

"Hey, Ryder."

She turned as a lumbering giant of a man hurried toward them. He tipped his cowboy hat to Danielle but didn't bother to wait for introductions.

"What's up, Buck?"

"There was a man come by the bank a few minutes ago looking for Langley. He was on the trail of a woman and, for some reason, he thought she might be in Kelman."

"Did he mention her name?" Ryder asked.

"Yep, he did. He said her name was Danielle Thibo…Thibo something. A Cajun name, I think." Buck turned and pointed. "That's him over there at the checkout counter. The guy with the brown hair and dark-rimmed glasses."

Danielle looked at the young man and struggled for breath. "Did he say why he was looking for the woman named Danielle?" she asked, her voice dry and scratchy.

"Yep." Buck pinned his gaze on her. "He said they'd had a lovers' quarrel and she'd run out on him. He's afraid something happened to her and he's awful anxious. She's his fiancée."

Chapter Three

Danielle stood in the sheriff's small office and tried to find something familiar about the stranger who was staring at her across the room. Ryder had taken over in the grocery store, introducing himself and instructing the man to meet them at Langley's office. If he hadn't, they might still be standing there. Her mind and body had refused to function. Even now, she found it difficult to breathe.

The man walked over and stopped in front of her. "What's wrong, Danielle? Why won't you look at me?"

"I'm sorry." She tried to say more, but her throat closed her words. The initial anxiety had been swallowed up by a cold, hard numbness that defied reason. She longed to find out who she was and yet all she could grasp was that this man who claimed to be her fiancé was a total stranger. "I don't remember you."

The man stared at her, doubt and confusion written all over his face. "I don't understand."

She all but fell into the chair a few inches behind her. "I don't even know your name," she murmured.

"It hasn't changed in the past three weeks. It's still Samuel Drummer." He turned back to Langley. "Where did she get those bruises on her face and arms? Has she been in an accident?''

''She was brutally attacked in New Orleans.''

''Oh, no.'' He knelt in front of Danielle, taking her hands in his. ''I should have known it was something like this when you didn't come home and didn't call. What were you doing in New Orleans?''

''I don't know.'' She studied the man's face, then stared into his eyes, hoping that she'd feel some spark of recognition, praying some fragment of recollection would flash into her brain. There was nothing. She pulled her hands from his.

He exhaled sharply. ''Help me, Danielle. It's so hard seeing you like this when I don't understand what's going on.''

''I'm sorry, Samuel. I'm not trying to be difficult. It's just that I'm having trouble remembering things. And people.'' She took a deep breath and forced the diagnosis from her dry throat. ''I have amnesia.''

''Amnesia.'' He stood and backed away as if she'd named some dread, contagious disease. ''Exactly how much do you remember?''

''Basically nothing. I don't even remember who I am.''

He dropped into the chair next to hers and buried his face in his hands. ''This is my fault,'' he mumbled. ''I knew you were upset. I should never have let you pack a bag and leave the house alone that night. I know how you are when you get that way.''

Langley leaned forward in his chair. ''Placing blame won't change anything. Danielle needs information about who she is. She needs your help in remembering her past.''

''Of course. I'll help all I can. I'll get her the best

doctors in Fort Worth. I'll take a night job if I have to in order to pay the bills.''

"She's seen a doctor. Facts are what we need now.''

"I'll tell you anything I can.'' He twisted his hands and stared at the toes of his brown loafers. "What do you want to know?''

Danielle scooted her chair around in order to face him. "I know my first name is Danielle. What's my last name?''

He hesitated. "Thibodeaux. Danielle Thibodeaux.''

A Cajun name. That explained her accent, but the name was no more familiar to her than the man who had said it. "Do I have a family?''

"Not anymore. You were an only child. Your parents are dead, at least that's what you told me. If there's anyone else, I don't know about them. I didn't even know about this Milton Maccabbe fellow whom you wanted to visit in Kelman until he started sending you letters. Frankly, I had my doubts about a man surfacing out of the blue and claiming to be your uncle.'' He straightened and stared at Danielle, his eyes flashing as if he'd just hit the jackpot. "That's it, isn't it? It's Milton Maccabbe. What did he do to you?''

Danielle's fingers dug into her palms. She unclasped her hands and ran them along the rough denim of her jeans. "Milton is dead, Samuel. He has been for two weeks now. He's not part of the problem.''

"At least he's not the one who attacked her,'' Langley corrected.

"Look, I'm sorry.'' Samuel shifted in his chair. "I didn't know.''

"How long have you known me, Samuel?''

"About six months. You moved to Fort Worth from some little town in south Louisiana. I met you in a club downtown. I bought you a drink. We danced a few times. You know how it is. We just hit it off.''

''What kind of work did I do?''

''You were unemployed when I met you, but you were looking for a job.''

''What kind of work was I looking for?''

''Waitressing. Or whatever you could find. You were low on funds.'' He stood and paced the small room. ''Look, we don't have to go into this now. I'll take you home. We'll get you medical care. You can rest in your own bed with your own things around you. I'll take care—''

Langley broke into his frantic rambling. ''We need Danielle's social security number, Samuel. Do you know it or know where we can find it?''

He stopped pacing. ''I don't have it. It's got to be in her purse. Did you check her driver's license?''

''My purse was stolen when I was mugged in New Orleans.''

Samuel threw up his hands in frustration. ''Of course, I should have realized. If you had your purse or even your luggage, you'd at least know your name and where you live.'' He raked his fingers through his hair. ''All this has taken me by such surprise. I mean, I never expected to run into anything like this.''

''You can't be any more confused than I am, Samuel,'' Danielle said.

''What about friends?'' Langley asked, breaking into the conversation. ''Did Danielle have any close friends?''

''Not in Fort Worth. She was…'' He hesitated. ''She stayed at home a lot after we moved in together. She was going through some hard times.''

''What kind of hard times?'' Langley tapped the

eraser end of a yellow pencil against the legal pad that rested at his fingertips. "Was she sick? Upset? Give me some specific details."

Samuel walked over and stood behind Danielle's chair. He dropped his hands possessively to her shoulders. "I don't see why we need to go into any of this right now. Danielle has been through enough. I'd just like to take her home."

"It's not quite that simple."

Samuel's grip on her shoulders tightened as his muscles tensed. "I'd like to know why the hell it isn't. I don't know what's going on here, but Danielle's obviously the victim, not the suspect. You can't hold her in this one-horse town."

Danielle felt they were talking as if she wasn't in the room, the same way she'd felt the first few days in the hospital. Then, she'd been too weak and confused to protest. She wasn't anymore. "I'm not being held here, Samuel. I'm staying of my own accord. And I'm not ready to go home with you. Not yet."

"I see." Samuel lifted his hands from her shoulders. "That's fine. If you want to stay here, I'll take a few more days off work and stay with you."

"There's one little complication there, Samuel." Langley rose from his chair and walked to the front of the desk. "The police believe the man who attacked Danielle might know her. The evidence suggests it could have been an estranged lover."

Samuel shook his head. "You surely don't suspect me. I don't have a violent bone in my body. Danielle can tell you that." He pushed his glasses up the bridge of his nose. "At least she could if she were herself."

"I'm not doubting you." Langley leveled a gaze at Samuel. "Not yet anyway. But for now, I think it's best if you see Danielle only when either I or the deputy can be present.''

Samuel's stance grew rigid. ''And what about you, Danielle? Is that the way you want it?''

Her heart went out to Samuel. It truly did. He seemed like a nice guy and genuinely frustrated. But he was still a stranger. And the New Orleans detective's theory still sent chills down her spine.

She considered her options. Go back to the Running Deer with Ryder and spend the day cleaning up a humongous mess. Or go back with Samuel and deal with feelings she was supposed to have for a man she didn't remember. Go back to the ranch and expect him to touch her with at least the familiarity he had shown in this room. Go back to the ranch and wonder if the man she was alone with was the one who'd tried to kill her.

An estranged husband. A jilted lover. The words of the New Orleans detective whirled in her mind.

''You didn't answer, Danielle.'' Samuel repeated his question, his tone bordering on pleading. ''What will it be?''

She took a deep breath and hoped she was making the right decision. ''I can't go with you, Samuel.'' She somehow managed to keep her voice steady. ''And I can't let you stay with me.''

Samuel started to argue. Langley cut him off.

''The lady said no, Mr. Drummer. If you have a problem with that, you'll have to take it up with me later. Right now, I'm going to have my brother drive Danielle back to the ranch she inherited and you and I are going to have a talk.''

Danielle observed the semipolite battle of wills being waged between the two men. With one of the men she felt a strange kinship, a trust, a feeling of security as if she had known him for a long time. The other man was a stranger, one whose touch disturbed her. The problem was her feelings seemed to have switched wires and attached to the wrong person.

She fought the impulse to bolt from this small, confining room and run out into the sunshine. For two weeks she'd known nothing but doubts and fears. The only reprieve she'd experienced had been the few hours she'd spent at the Burning Pear.

Langley, Ryder, Mary, even little Betsy, the unofficial Randolph. From them emanated a warmth that reached clear to the frigid chill that had settled in her soul. And Samuel Drummer, no matter what he had meant to her in the past, didn't project that kind of warmth. Worse, she didn't have the strength to give him the attention he obviously wanted and probably deserved.

Ryder picked that moment to knock on the door, or more likely, Langley had instructed him when to show up. He ambled inside, sporting his cocky smile and tipping his black Stetson. The tension diminished appreciably. Evidently, Samuel realized that he was outnumbered by Randolphs, and that no matter how guilty he made her feel, she wasn't about to walk out of the office with him.

She might be sorry later that she hadn't gone with Samuel. But the only thing she could depend on now was her instinct for survival.

Langley walked to the door as she and Ryder were leaving. She looked up and their gazes locked. Strange, but the look they shared was far more intimate than the touch Samuel had attempted, and yet she didn't draw away. He was part of a new life, the only life she could remember. He'd become part of the world she was trying to fit into.

"I'll come by the Running Deer when I'm through here," he said. "In the meantime, you're in good hands with Ryder."

"I know. I just chose a mop at the store that will fit his 'good hands' perfectly."

"Then I'll hurry. I want to be there in time to see my little brother wield it."

She walked out the door. All of a sudden, even the mess at the Running Deer seemed like a welcome change.

LANGLEY TRIED the hotel room in Hawaii where Branson was staying one more time. No answer. Finally, a computerized voice came on the line and told him to punch one if he wanted to leave a message.

He didn't bother. He'd already left a message, one of quiet desperation.

He'd checked out the info Samuel Drummer had given him. He'd verified the man's address, his phone number, his social security number. He lived in Fort Worth, just as he'd said. He had a checking account, a job as a traveling salesman, a car payment that he was usually late in making. In short, Samuel Drummer existed.

Danielle was a different story. She had no employer except Samuel, who claimed she helped with his sales reports and record-keeping. She had no landlord and no friends he could locate. Worst of all, he could find no social security number that would make it easier to run a paper trail on her.

But the fact that kept gnawing in Langley's gut was the detective's theory that Danielle's attacker had probably known her, that the attack had been too vicious for a mugging gone bad. Judging from what he'd learned from the hospital, he would have come to that same conclusion.

And if he found out Samuel Drummer was the man who'd stabbed Danielle and left her to die on a back street in New Orleans, heaven help him.

Badge or not, Langley was a man, and a man could only stomach so much. He stood up, sending his chair careering backward in the process. He had to get out of Branson's office for a while, get out of town and see some wide open spaces. Grabbing his hat, he shoved it down on his head and strode out the door.

He crawled behind the wheel of his truck and started the engine. Without even thinking about it, he headed for the outskirts of Kelman and the highway that led toward the Burning Pear. Only he knew that this time it wasn't his own ranch that was pulling him in that direction.

He was going to the Running Deer. But he had one stop to make first.

DANIELLE SCRUBBED the kitchen wall with a vengeance. Her fingernails were chipped, her hands chapped from strong cleansers, her hair falling from one of Milton's bandannas that she'd used to bind her flyaway curls into a ponytail.

Stopping to rest, she sucked in a deep breath. The injuries she'd received in New Orleans were still taking their toll, but in spite of aching muscles, she felt better than she had since the assault. Physical labor was obviously good for the soul if not the muscles.

And once she'd gotten started, there was no place to stop. The sofa, recliner, mattress, pillows—in short, every place Milton might have hidden something of value—all had been gutted. The kitchen cabinets had been cleared with abandon, as if someone had just raked his hand across the shelves and sent the contents flying.

But there were still quite a few dishes that hadn't been broken, as well as a nice supply of canned goods in the pantry. Ryder had made several trips back to the big house at Burning Pear to pick up cleaning supplies, and every time he returned, he'd been loaded with food items Mary thought she might need. On the last trip, he'd even turned up with a sleeping bag and a couple of quilts to ease the discomfort of sleeping on the floor.

She could stay there for a while if it came to that. Of course, there were still some legal details to settle. But Langley had said he would look into the records that had been filed with the courts. It was possible that Milton had put the ranch in her name before he died or that he had filed a will.

As soon as everything was legal, she'd sell the ranch. She couldn't stay there. Even though she didn't remember anything specific about her life, she did remember how to do certain things. But absolutely nothing came to mind when she looked at cattle. They were big, especially the bulls. Ryder had pointed out a couple on their way back to the ranch.

She wasn't exactly sure what a rancher did with bulls, but whatever it was, she had no intention of tackling that chore. Not unless you could do it from the other side of the rows of prickly barbed wire.

Bending over, she dipped her cleaning rag back into the bucket of warm, sudsy water and wrung it nearly dry. One more section of wall and the kitchen would be finished. Two rooms down. It was a start.

She broke into a song, amazed that her uncooperative mind could locate lyrics when it couldn't retrieve personal facts. And even more amazed that she felt like singing.

She belted one out. No use worrying about disturbing the neighbors. There weren't any.

A round of appreciative applause sounded behind her and she jerked around, expecting to see Ryder. Instead, it was Langley who stepped through the door.

"Excuse me, Bonnie Raitt, but I was looking for a woman named Danielle Thibodeaux."

"Bonnie Raitt. Now that rings a bell. A singer, right?"

"You got it."

"Go figure." She dropped her rag into the pail of gray water and wiped her hands on the legs of her jeans. "How long have you been standing there?"

"Long enough to decide you're the best-looking cleaning woman I've ever come across."

His compliment took her by surprise. But this time she didn't blush or feel ill at ease. The truth was, she liked the way he was looking at her, as if she was an attractive woman and not some medical specimen in a science project.

"You're efficient, too." He glanced appreciatively around. "I can't believe what you've done with the kitchen."

"Ryder helped. Mostly, we just hauled out the trash, but we did enough scrubbing to earn a few blisters."

"Where's Ryder now?"

"He's out back, hosing down the kitchen chairs. But he's told me more than once that cleaning house is not fitting work for a previous World Rodeo Champion."

"Oh, he did, did he? Did he also tell you he's going bonkers sitting this year out while his knee heals? Apparently, life at the Burning Pear is not quite as exciting as life on the suicide circuit.''

She laughed, and the sound of it took her by surprise. It was a new experience. A nice one.

"Lacks excitement. I believe Ryder did mention that," she said. "Something about a crying baby and bellowing calves, and a severe shortage of beautiful women."

"That's Ryder. Ride 'em and rope 'em, and love 'em and leave 'em. He's made a career of all the above."

Nice, easy talk, but sooner or later they had to get back to the business at hand. She decided on sooner. "So how did the second half of the meeting with Samuel go?"

"About like the first half. Apparently, he didn't learn a lot about your past life during the six months you were together. He says you were given to sudden irrational mood swings and periods of depression. Other than that, you were Miss Wonderful."

Twinges of apprehension dampened Danielle's good spirits. She was sorry she'd asked about Samuel. It brought all her concerns to the forefront once more. Had she been in love with Samuel? Had she run out on him? Had he found her in New Orleans with another man and gone berserk?

The images were ugly, depressing. Maybe the psychiatrist was right. Perhaps she'd chosen to forget her past because it was just too grim to face.

"I didn't mean to upset you," Langley said.

"You didn't. The situation does. Or maybe I'm just having one of those irrational mood swings."

"I'd say you're having a normal reaction to stress and frustration."

Their eyes met across the room. She had a sudden

urge to run to him, beg him to hold her close, pretend for a minute that the rugged cowboy with the strong arms was the fiancé from her past.

If he felt the same urge, he gave no sign. Instead, he turned and stepped back into the living room. A minute later, he reappeared with a large, gift-wrapped box in his hand. "I bought you a present."

"It's not my birthday."

"It might be." His eyes were teasing now. "Open it."

Excitement tickled her senses. She started to tug at the ribbon, then stopped. She shouldn't accept it. It would change the relationship, make Langley more than just a man looking out for a woman in need.

But the relationship had already changed. She'd met his family, spent the night in his home. She finished unwrapping the package and set the box on the table. Then she lifted the lid and pulled back a square of white tissue.

She reached inside and drew out a cowboy hat. Charcoal-gray felt. "It's beautiful," she said, trying it on. "The first present I ever remember getting."

"Then I'm glad I'm the one who bought it for you."

"But why did you buy it?"

"You're a rancher now. You should look like one. Besides, I thought you might need a little cheering up. You've had nothing but bad news since you arrived in Kelman."

Danielle laid the hat on the table. "I appreciate this, Langley. I really do, but you shouldn't have done this."

"You can take it back if you don't like it or if it doesn't fit."

"It's not that. It's just that…" She paused, drowning in the awkward moment. She ran a finger along the line of stitching that edged the hat's brim. "You know I can't get involved with you. Even if I wanted to, I couldn't. I can't think about relationships until I know who I really am."

Now she'd made him nervous. He rammed his hands deep into his front pockets. "I'm not aiming to get involved with you or anyone else, Danielle. So if that's what you're thinking, you can set your mind at ease. And even if I was, I wouldn't think you could be bought for a hat."

She nodded, feeling like a first-class chump for reading seduction designs into his neighborly acts. "Let's start over. I thank you for the gift and the help."

"You're welcome. Actually, I went a step further than buying the hat. I talked to Debbie Griffith down at Kelman's only department store. She's agreed to open an account for you. If you intend to get out and explore the ranch, you'll need some ranch wear. Boots, extra shirts and jeans and a light jacket. It gets cool this time of year when the sun goes down. Occasionally, it gets downright cold."

"I was wondering why there was a fireplace in the cabin."

"There's no central heat. I told you, the place is rustic." He reached over and adjusted the tilt of her hat. "Anyway, you can get what you need and pay for it after the ranch is officially in your name and you sell a few head of cattle. Or after your memory returns and you get access to your own bank account."

"Ms. Griffith is very accommodating." And Danielle knew the reason. Langley had agreed to make good on what she owed in the event she ran out on the debt. She just wasn't sure why, especially since he apparently had no interest in fostering an intimate relationship with her.

It was hard to imagine that neighbors were this friendly, even in Kelman, Texas.

Langley picked up the wrapping from the gift and wadded it into a ball. He tossed it into a plastic garbage bag by the back door. ''Getting you the right clothes to wear will be the easy part. The legal documents that give you the right to be on this property may be a little more difficult to come by.'' His tone had changed from neighborly to serious.

''I have a last name now. Danielle Thibodeaux. There have to be records of my existence.''

Langley propped his backside against the counter. ''I'd like to think so, but so far I haven't found any. I spent the afternoon running unsuccessful computer searches with the help of the deputy and a buddy with the state troopers. What we really need is a social security number.''

''Where does that leave me, Langley? All I have is a letter saying I'm inheriting a ranch from an uncle I don't remember. Will you be coming over here one day soon to evict me and send me back to Samuel Drummer?''

Langley's eyes cooled to a frosted gray. ''I have no evidence to link Samuel to your attack, Danielle. I have a call in to my brother in Hawaii, but I feel sure he's going to tell me that I have no legal grounds for keeping Samuel away from you.''

''So if he's the man who attacked me, he would be free to strike again.''

''Unless you go through the courts and get a restraining order.''

Memories surfaced in her mind, the same sort of sporadic, incomplete images that had haunted her for the past two weeks. They appeared without any warning.

The blood. The pain. The man's eyes as he hammered his fist into her face.

She swayed and Langley caught her, holding her trembling body in his strong arms. But even Langley wouldn't be able to save her forever. She didn't know if Samuel had been the one who attacked her, but judging from the message she'd found in the cabin, there was a good chance the man who'd left her for dead in New Orleans had been at the ranch. He would return. If not in person, then in every nightmare that visited her in the lonely bedroom of an isolated cabin at Running Deer.

Pushing away from Langley, she forced herself to stand on her own. This was no time to lose her willpower. She stuck a hand in her pocket, and her fingers raked the edge of the key Milton had sent her. A note and a key, but she'd tried the key today. It didn't fit the door.

She closed her eyes as a new image flickered across her mind. The strength of it was staggering, like a slap of cold wind blowing away the dark shadows. She pulled the key from her pocket and stared at it.

"What is it, Danielle? You look as if you've seen a ghost."

"No. It's the key that Milton sent me."

"What about it?"

"I think I know what it's for."

Chapter Four

Langley stood silently, watching as Danielle kept staring at the brass key in her hand. She was pale and shaking, a transformation that had overcome her in mere seconds.

"The key fits a metal box, Langley. There's something inside the box that Milton wants me to have."

Langley put a hand to the small of her back. "Take it easy, Danielle. Let's go out to the porch and get some fresh air."

"I don't need fresh air. I'm a little shaken, but I'm not ill."

"You're not yourself."

"How would you know?" She stepped away from him. "The point is that I finally remember something worthwhile. I was standing here talking to you and then, clear as day, I could hear a man's voice telling me that I was to use the key to open a metal box."

"You were hearing voices?" His own anxiety level skyrocketed. "What exactly do you mean by voices?"

She rubbed her temple. "It's bizarre, I know, but it's happened more than once over the past two weeks. I'll be doing something and a memory will flash across my mind. Only it's not really like a memory. It's as if the event were happening all over again."

He was still concerned. Not that he knew beans about amnesia, but hearing voices didn't sound like a good thing. "Does it usually come in the form of voices?"

"No, but perhaps my uncle phoned me and told me about the key and the ranch before he mailed the letter. I may have been remembering his phone call."

"If you're right, the metal box may contain the will."

"It may. Only something in the memory frightened me, raised the hairs on my neck, sent a shiver up my spine."

"Is that the way it usually works when you have one of these…?"

"Flashbacks. Visions. Memories. You can say whatever you're thinking, Langley, but the answer is no. Usually when the memories rush in, there's a sense of relief, like a few minutes ago when I remembered who Bonnie Raitt was. But sometimes they make me uneasy the way that one did. And if they're related to the attack, I always taste the fear."

She started pacing. The movement eased Langley's mind a little. Her steps were steady, and the color was returning to her face.

"That might explain why someone tried to kill me a couple of weeks ago," she said, stopping to lean against the kitchen table. "And why he doesn't want me at the ranch. The person who's trying to get rid of me could be looking for the metal box. Judging from the destruction, he may have already found it."

"Don't jump to conclusions. We can't even be certain the attack on your life and the message left on the mirror are related. There's still a chance that the attack in New Orleans actually was a random mugging."

"And there's a chance it's going to snow today, but I'm not buying a sled."

He put out his hand. "Let me look at the key."

She handed it to him. He studied it closely, then ran a thumb down the serrations. It was small, the kind that would fit a medium-size padlock—one that could be picked up at any variety or hardware store.

Danielle walked over to stand beside him. "No part of the house was untouched, Langley. If the box was here, then whoever vandalized the place must have found it."

"In which case, there was no reason for him to leave you a warning." Langley ran the possibilities through his mind. "A ranch is more than a house, and especially so in Milton's case. He spent most of his days outside and some of his nights."

"But if it's not in the house, it could be anywhere."

"Exactly."

Danielle rubbed the back of her neck. "It's so frustrating. I catch a scrap of memory, just enough to torment me and not enough to do any good."

"Even a scrap has to be a good sign. That means your memory is returning. When it does, you'll be able to remember the entire conversation with Milton. If there is a box, you'll be able to go right to it."

"And if there's not a box, then I'm just another fruitcake hearing voices. Is that what you think, Langley? I wouldn't blame you if you did. Sometimes I'm afraid of that myself."

Langley took her hands in his. He did it without thinking, but awareness was immediate and overwhelming. He dropped her hands and stepped away.

"I don't think you're crazy, Danielle. I think you're a woman struggling with a difficult situation. I also think you're in danger. That's why I can't let you stay here alone."

"I can't move in with your family, Langley. It's not fair to your mother or to Ryder."

"Then I'll have some of my men take turns watching your place when you're here alone. I don't want you on the ranch by yourself until we know exactly what's going on and who's responsible for the trouble."

Langley glanced up as Ryder came through the front door, toting a chair in each hand.

"So, you finally made it out here, oh helpful brother, just as the work is finished." Ryder dropped both chairs with a clatter.

"Right. I always did have good timing." A lie, but it sounded good. His timing right now with regard to romantic feelings was certainly way off.

Ryder pushed the chairs under the edge of the table. "Don't let him fool you, Danielle. That used to be my line, up until the time some fool hit-and-run driver came racing into me and dang near killed me. As it was, he banged up my knee so bad it predicts rain more accurately than the National Weather Service."

Danielle turned to Ryder. "Is that how you hurt your leg? I just assumed it was a rodeo accident."

"No, but I'd feel a lot better if it had been. Then I'd at least have a good story to tell."

"I've never known that to stop you," Langley said. "But it looks like you and Danielle both did more work than talking around here today."

"The woman's a slave driver," Ryder said, sticking out his hands as if their condition would prove his statement. "But if you're through playing lawman for the day, you might take Danielle riding before dinner, teach her that ranching is more than housework. I checked Milton's tack room. He's got everything you'd need.

And a horseman like him was bound to own good riding stock.''

Danielle propped her hands on her shapely hips. ''Don't even think about it. I only ride things that come equipped with seat belts.''

''What kind of rancher are you?'' Langley teased.

''A live one who plans to stay that way. I've had enough adventure lately.''

''There's no such thing as enough adventure,'' Ryder said. ''But there is definitely such a thing as too much work. I'm getting out of here before you find something more for me to do. Besides, it's Langley's turn to stick his hands in dirty water.''

Danielle thanked Ryder again for the help. Langley walked out to the truck with him, filling him in on the details of the afternoon.

''I like her,'' Ryder said, obviously referring to Danielle, ''but she falls into some funny moods.''

''I think it's the amnesia.''

''Yeah, I guess. Still, it seems strange she didn't remember anything about Samuel this morning.''

''I wasn't so surprised at that. She doesn't remember anyone from her past, but a few minutes ago, she all but fell into a trance. I put a call into the New Orleans psychiatrist this afternoon, the one who treated her while she was in the hospital. Hopefully, he'll return the call soon. I'd like to get his take on her reactions.''

''That's a good idea. I know you want to help her, but amnesia is serious. You wouldn't want to do anything to stand in the way of her recovery.''

''I'm not a doctor. That's for sure. Mostly I just want to keep her safe.''

''I know. It somehow seems to me that if she was in

love with Samuel before the amnesia, she'd feel something around him.''

Langley stepped over a muddy spot where Ryder had been hosing the chairs. ''Are you an expert on love, little brother?''

''I know it's damn hard to forget someone you care about.'' Ryder opened the truck door but didn't get in. ''And while we're on that subject, I think Danielle likes you. She's a super-looking lady, but I'd be careful about getting involved with her.''

''I'm just doing the job I told Branson I'd do, Ryder. I'm not here to try to get the new neighbor lady in bed.''

''Be careful. That's all I'm saying.''

Langley stood and watched until the cloud of dust had settled behind the disappearing truck. Ryder didn't have to worry about him. Even if he wanted to get involved with Danielle, he couldn't, not with her living under a cloak of confusion as dense as the dust Ryder's truck had stirred up.

She already had a life, one she would eventually remember and return to. A life in which he played no part. Still, he could show her the ranch. And if she didn't want to see the sprawling acres on horseback, there was another way.

''ONCE WE'RE UP IN THE AIR, you'll love it.''

Danielle stared at the helicopter and struggled to hear Langley's reassurances over the swishing sound of the rotor blades and the roar of the engine. ''And to think I turned down a horse ride because I thought it was dangerous.''

''You said your only requirement was seat belts.''

''Next time I'll be more specific.'' Her pulse quickened. When Langley had offered the ''seat-belt'' tour of the ranch, she'd expected it to be in his pickup truck, not a sassy little helicopter. But instead of driving her around the Running Deer, he'd driven her to the Burning Pear and a much more adventuresome form of transportation.

Sucking in a healthy gulp of air, she took Langley's outstretched hand and clambered into the passenger seat, acutely aware that her feet would not be touching the ground again any time soon.

"Would you like the door on or off?"

"Tell me you're joking." But one look at his side of the copter and she knew he was deadly serious. The opening was unobstructed. "I want my door *on.* Definitely on. And I'd like all the other helicopter body parts on, as well."

"There you go, denying your spirit of adventure again."

"I left it in New Orleans."

Reaching for the strap of the seat belt, she adjusted it over her shoulder and snapped the buckle into place. Once snapped, she tried it just to make sure it held.

"Are you ready for takeoff?" Langley asked, climbing into the small cockpit beside her.

"I think so." She peered out the side window. "I hope you're licensed to fly this whirling contraption."

"Licensed and experienced. The helicopter is the fastest and most efficient way to get around the ranch. I even use it to round up cattle, though I call in an extra pilot and chopper for roundup chores."

"The modern rancher. What about the poor horses? Don't you need them anymore?"

He slapped a hand over his heart as if she'd wounded him. "A cowboy will always need his horse."

She couldn't keep from smiling as Langley lifted the

craft off the ground. Still, the butterflies in her stomach took flight with them, all wings fluttering at once before settling into a holding pattern as the copter leveled off and headed west.

They crossed a small creek and a fence line, wooden posts and barbed wire, all set in an unbelievably straight line. "When will we get to the Running Deer?"

"We're here. I looked up the boundaries today at the courthouse. You own three thousand acres. That's small by south Texas standards, but it's plenty to run your cattle."

Her cattle. *Her* land.

Exhilaration danced inside her, made her dizzy. She was floating above acres of wide-open spaces that might actually belong to her. No wonder men like Langley grew so attached to this way of life. She shaded her eyes to get a better look at movement on the ground below her.

"Look. Is that a jackrabbit?"

"It is. They're plentiful around here, some of them huge."

"That one could pass for a kangaroo."

Langley laughed. The sound was easy. Being with him was easy. Of course, with the rest of her life on a collision course with disaster, "easy" was a relative term.

"There's a couple of deer down there. Can you see them? They're just to the left of that windmill."

She directed her gaze to the area where he was pointing. Two deer raced in front of them, their heads high, their movements as graceful as a choreographed dance.

"Oh, they're beautiful. But we're frightening them."

"They'll be okay. They'll run until they can't hear us anymore, then they'll settle back down. Their real problems will start when deer season opens. Some of the ranchers lease out part of their land to hunting clubs. Milton didn't.''

"Good for him.''

"Don't give him too much credit. He wasn't opposed to hunting. He just didn't want any strangers on his land.''

"More of his unsocial ways, I guess.'' Danielle leaned forward, losing her nervousness to the thrill of the flight and her fascination with the scenery.

The land was flat, an unending plain of sparse grass, cacti, scrubby trees and an assortment of wildlife and cattle. If she'd ever seen anything like it before, the memory was lost like most of her others, fallen into the black hole called amnesia.

"Look, there's another creek.'' She pointed at a meandering line of grayish water beneath them.

"Actually, that one's a river. In south Texas, we're generous with naming our water sources. If it's wet most of the year, we usually call it a river.''

"Are there fish in it?''

"You can catch a mess for dinner most any day you have the time. See that lean-to over there? Your uncle used to set up camp there and fish for two or three days at a time. I'd see his campfires sometime when I was out working my own cattle.''

"He really was a loner, wasn't he?''

"More than ever the last few months of his life. I imagine he was coming to grips with the prospect of dying, and maybe with himself.''

"I wish I'd been here for him. It must have been sad dying with few friends and no family.''

"I'd think it would be even sadder to *live* that way.''

They flew for a while without talking, the silence between them broken only by the whirring of the helicopter. Danielle couldn't help but think that the lack of conversation between them was equally as comfortable as talking had been. Strange that she found Langley so easy to be with when her encounter with Samuel had been rife with tension. But then, Langley hadn't shared a past with her, a past she didn't remember.

Langley dropped altitude until they flew just over the top of a leaning chimney. "That was the Simpson place years ago," he said, slowing and then turning for her to get a better look. "They owned this land back before I was born. See, you can still make out the remnants of the dirt road Mr. Simpson used to get out here."

"What happened to the house?"

"It got caught up in a brushfire. A lot of the old houses around here have been lost to them. They spread so quickly in the wind."

"But some of the walls and part of the roof are still standing. I'm surprised the Simpsons never rebuilt."

"They built a much larger place just west of town. Kincaid bought this land. He owned it up until he deeded it to your uncle."

"Joshua Kincaid. His name keeps coming up."

"He's that kind of guy. His fingers manage to find their way into lots of pies. My brother Dillon's convinced that not all of them are legal." Langley turned west, following another meandering strand of water.

"Is that another river?"

"No, that's Branson Creek. There's a great picnic spot near here. I'll have to take you there sometime."

"Good. I love picnics. At least I think I do." She spotted another building, this one with three sides and a sagging roof. "Is that another home?"

"No, that used to be a barn. It probably hasn't been

used in twenty-five years. There are a lot of decaying structures like that around here. Most of them house scorpions and spiders and little else. There are some abandoned wells hereabouts, too. Those you need to watch out for. They're supposed to be covered, but every so often someone stumbles into one that isn't.''

Danielle stretched, easing the strain on muscles that had been under too much stress lately. In spite of the anxiety she'd felt when she boarded the helicopter, she felt calmer than she had since the attack. Even the sky was doing its part. The glaring rays of the afternoon sun had softened to glorious hues of orange and gold as the sun sank toward the horizon.

"I'm glad you insisted I come for the ride, Langley."

"I thought it might do you good. You get a whole different perspective from a few yards above the tree-tops."

"I need a new perspective. The only problem is I realize now how hopeless it would be to try to search the entire ranch for a small metal box."

"I'd say it's impossible unless we have some idea where to start looking. But once your memory returns, you can go right to it."

"*When* my memory returns. Which might be never." She could see Langley's truck and the roof of the Randolph home not far ahead. The tour was almost over. Her stomach stayed in the sky as Langley made the descent and brought the helicopter to the ground in the clearing north of his ranch. He adjusted the controls, then killed the engine.

"But we did make progress today," he said. "Now that we know your last name, it should be easy to prove that you're Milton's only living relative. I checked with Dillon this afternoon. He says that's all you really need to inherit the ranch. A will is helpful, but it isn't always necessary in that situation.''

"We also know that I have to be the Danielle that Milton sent the letter to. Otherwise Samuel would never have known to come to Kelman looking for me. Langley, that's it.'' She grabbed his arm, excitement surging inside her. "If I told Samuel about the letter, I may have told him about the phone call from Milton, as well. I may have told him about the metal box. He may know where to find it.''

"It's worth a try. I can go with you to the hotel. That's where he said he'd be if you needed him.''

She considered the offer. Having Langley beside her would make it easier for her, but it might make it more difficult for Samuel. "I think I should go by myself, Langley. I'll take Milton's old truck and have Samuel meet me at Gus's. That way I won't feel threatened, and Samuel won't feel like you're about to arrest him.''

"If that's the way you want it.''

Her response had annoyed Langley. She had no idea why, but there was no denying the irritation that colored his Texas drawl. "It's not that I don't appreciate your help,'' she said, hoping he'd understand. "I just think it would go better that way.''

"I'm sure you're right.'' He jumped out, and she followed suit, opening her door and sliding to the ground. "I'll drive you home,'' he said, leading the way to his truck. "Then, if you like, I'll drive you into town and drop you off at Gus's. I'm not sure I'd trust Milton's old truck to get you there and back.''

"Tomorrow will be soon enough,'' she said, deciding that a good night's sleep was much more inviting than a conversation with Samuel.

"That's probably a good idea. You've had a long day."

"Long, but good. The best one in two weeks."

He stopped at the passenger-side door of the truck and opened it for her. "And now you've had a bird's-eye view of your ranch. That should give you a good start into your new life."

A new life.

The idea pummeled her mind as she settled in for the short ride home. She had fallen into a life. She just wasn't sure it was hers.

She owned a ranch, but she wasn't a rancher. She'd had a lover, but she didn't know him. She had a key, but no lock to open. And the neighbor filling in as sheriff had become her friend, though she wasn't sure he'd still want to be after she regained her memory. And even if he did, she'd probably be engaged to Samuel Drummer and living in Fort Worth.

She wrapped her arms around her chest and stared out the window. The sun was slipping fast below the horizon and the air had grown cooler. It would soon be dark. It would also be the first night she'd spent alone in two weeks. The first one since—

She pushed the frightening images away. They would not be good company when she was all alone in her uncle's cabin tonight. And she was suddenly very thankful that Langley was sending over one of his hands to keep watch

DANIELLE DRAGGED HERSELF across the bare wooden floor of the living room and into the kitchen, so tired she ached to collapse somewhere and fall asleep. In fact, if the living room had offered a piece of furniture to collapse on, she might have dropped there and foregone dinner altogether.

But the only living-room chair that had survived the brutal vandalism was a wooden one that tilted to the left when she sat in it. She sniffed as she opened the refrigerator. In spite of all the cleaning, there was still a fishy smell. She'd have to cover everything she put in there. The house had a lingering odor, as well, one that hovered over everything like invisible silt.

She'd have to air out the place and buy a supply of air fresheners and candles. Rummaging through the few groceries she'd bought and the extras Ryder had hauled over from the Burning Pear, she decided on a hot ham sandwich. It would be quick and easy.

In seconds, she had dropped a couple of slices of the honey-cured ham into a small iron skillet. She retrieved a plastic cup from the cabinet and poured it full of cold milk, then chose a small tin saucer just big enough for her sandwich.

The simple life. Amazingly enough, the lack of frills didn't daunt her. Perhaps she wasn't used to a lot more. She forked a slice of ham to turn it, but stopped in midturn. A shuffling sound had come from the bedroom.

She heard it again, louder this time, and clearly from the bedroom. The fork and ham tumbled from her hand, falling noisily to the range and bouncing onto the floor. "Who's there?"

The words were a husky whisper, caught in her dry throat. She didn't wait for an answer. Instead, she jerked open a drawer and pulled out a butcher knife.

"Who's—"

She didn't finish her question. She didn't have to. Samuel Drummer stepped through the bedroom door and into the small kitchen.

"Don't look at me like that, Danielle. I came all the way from Fort Worth to find you. Surely you knew I wasn't going to leave Kelman without getting what I came for.''

Chapter Five

Samuel's words set Danielle's nerves on edge. Her grip tightened on the knife. "What are you talking about?"

He turned his head from one side to the other, his gaze sliding around the room, then lingering on the vase of wildflowers in the middle of the kitchen table. "I'm talking about you and me. I'm talking about the fact that I want you to come home with me."

"And I will, as soon as the amnesia lifts and I remember our life together."

"What will you do until then? You can't stay here in this run-down shack. Not after what you've been through. Get your things and come back to the hotel with me. I won't leave here without you."

"How did you get out here, Samuel? There's no car in the driveway."

"I parked it in the back and out of sight. I figured you were out with that cowboy who's sniffing around you like a dog after a bone. I can't talk to you with him around. He twists my words. That's why you need to come into town with me. I can help you."

She stepped to the range and turned off the gas. "Langley's not here now, Samuel. We can talk."

"Not unless you put that knife away. You make me

feel like a criminal. I've never hurt you, Danielle. I never would. All I've ever done is love you. I don't know why you don't believe me.''

"I want to believe you, Samuel. I really do. It's just that without memories of my past, we're strangers." She forked the slices of ham onto the saucer, but her appetite had vanished.

"You're not a stranger to me. I know everything about you. The way you like your eggs. The way you can sleep through anything. The way you look forward to a night out on the town." He laid his hand on her shoulder. "All that and so much more."

The "so much more" was what worried her. There was no way she could even think about going to the hotel with Samuel. No way she could think of intimacy with a stranger. She pulled away. "Please don't touch me. Not yet."

He shook his head, a scowl twisting his lips. "Okay. I've been practically crazy the past three weeks, not knowing where you were and if you were safe. But I'll deal with it. At least now I know why you didn't call or come home."

Danielle tried to keep the conversation focused. "You said I was upset when I left. What was I upset about?"

"You wanted to get married right away. I wanted to wait. But I don't care anymore. I just want you back."

His words tore at her resolve. He seemed so genuine. But still her doubts persisted. "Why didn't you come for me sooner, Samuel? Why didn't you go to New Orleans and search for me?"

"Believe me, if I'd had any idea where you were, I would have been there. You told me you had to get away to think about us. I never dreamed you'd go back to Louisiana. Then when you didn't come home, I didn't know who to call. I didn't know where to look. Finally, in desperation, I tried Kelman. Thank God that I did."

"And marriage was the only issue between us?"

He shook his head. "No, you thought I worked too much, that I left you alone too often."

"What kind of job do you have?"

"I sell commercial cleaning supplies. I'm out of town most weeks from Monday through Friday. I put in long hours, but I'm trying to save for a down payment on a house."

"I should understand that."

"You should, but you're…temperamental, a little insecure." He smiled and reached up to tuck a wayward strand of hair behind her ear. "Which always surprises me, considering you're so beautiful and that I totally adore you."

"Temperamental and insecure and I get angry when you do your job. I can certainly see why you're crazy about me."

"Love makes a fool of me."

Danielle laid down the knife, still confused but unafraid. "Are there any good things about me?"

"You like to have fun. Dancing, drinking, going out on the town. And when we make love, you take me to the moon." He pulled her to him, so close his chest touched the tips of her breasts.

Impulsively, she backed away. Two weeks ago, she might have been in love with him, but those memories were lost. All she felt now was a tangle of unfamiliar emotions that clashed and grappled in her mind. She trembled and closed her eyes.

"You can't even bear to look at me, can you? Do you have any idea how that makes me feel, how much it hurts?"

She opened her eyes and forced herself to meet his gaze. "I'm sorry, Samuel." She brushed her bangs from her face. "I seem to say that a lot lately."

"There's no need to be sorry. You're confused. I understand that. I just don't want you to shut me out. I want to help you."

"Why don't you sit down?" She motioned to one of the kitchen chairs, then dropped into the nearest one herself. "I need to ask you about something."

He sat, never taking his eyes off her. "You know I'd do anything to help. The sooner you regain your memory, the better it will be for us."

"Did I ever mention to you that my uncle had sent me a key?"

"A key to what?"

"I'm not sure. Maybe a metal box."

"No. The only thing you told me was that the old man wanted to see you before he died."

"Then I didn't tell you he was leaving me the ranch?"

"If you had, I would have known the guy was crazy. You didn't even know the man. That's why I can't understand your wanting to stay here instead of going home with me."

Home with Samuel. Uneasiness churned inside her again. He was attractive and nice enough, but she couldn't visualize talking to him over breakfast or lying in his arms at night.

He got up from his chair and rounded the table. Stepping behind her, he leaned over and began kneading the knotted muscles in her neck and shoulders. "If you won't come home with me, let me stay here with you, Danielle. Let me take care of you."

"I can't do that, Samuel. I need time by myself. Actually, I'm so tired tonight I can barely think straight.

It's been a very long day. It would be better if you left now so I can get some sleep."

"But I couldn't rest with you here all by yourself. If you don't want me in the house, I'll stay in the bunkhouse. You can't object to that."

A warning flag went up in her mind. "You've never been to the Running Deer before. How do you know there's a bunkhouse?"

He pushed his glasses higher on his nose. "I just assumed there was. Don't all ranches have a bunkhouse?"

Of course. She was overreacting. The paranoia brought on by amnesia. "I'm sorry, Samuel. You could stay in the bunkhouse, but it's occupied by some of the hands who are running the ranch." She was lying. Langley had said he'd send someone over to watch the cabin, but he hadn't said a thing about using the bunkhouse. But she didn't want Samuel that close, didn't want to have to face him again in the morning. And lying seemed better than hurting his feelings even more than she already had.

She walked to the front door and pushed it open, but Samuel balked at leaving, his face drawn, his eyes narrowed. "You really don't want me around, do you? By the time you change your mind, it just may be too late. A man can only take so much rejection."

"Maybe you should go back to Fort Worth for now."

"Are you trying to get rid of me? Because I'm telling you this loud and clear. If you run me off, I won't be back." He stamped past her and out the door. She closed it behind him and leaned against it, not breathing easy until the drone of his car engine faded into the distance.

She tried to imagine the life he described. Partying, arguing over his work hours, making love. But her feelings for him were buried too deep, locked away in some chamber she couldn't find. One day, she might remember and want him back in her life. Tonight, she just wanted sleep.

THE SUN WAS BARELY UP when Langley strode into the small sheriff's office the next morning. He'd planned to go back to the office last night after he'd left Danielle, but he'd taken a couple of emergency calls instead. Nothing serious, but time-consuming all the same.

Gordon turned as the door swung open. "You're in early." The young deputy finished dumping the used coffee grounds into the trash as he greeted Langley. "Is something up?"

"I hope not. I'd like a nice, quiet day. How was your shift?"

"Damn near perfect. Only call I had was from Mrs. Clifford. She wanted me to lock George up 'cause one of his buddies brought him home drunk again."

"Was he causing problems?"

"Not unless you call passing out on the front porch a problem. I helped her get him to bed and told her I'd talk to him tonight when he was sober. I'll let you have that chore if you want it."

"Not me. From the looks of Branson's desk, I've got more than enough waiting."

"Yeah. Calamity said you got a passel of phone calls yesterday afternoon. None of them were emergencies, so she just left you messages."

Calamity. It wasn't her real name, but it fitted her well. No wonder her family had pinned it on her a long time ago. She was a redheaded spitfire of a middle-aged woman Branson had hired recently to take care of office duties.

According to Branson, if you left her in the office by herself too long, you'd always come back to trouble. She riled more folks than she helped, telling them whether or not she thought their problems were worthy of the sheriff's attention. And she didn't hesitate to give the caller her two cents worth on any problem they had.

But she apparently saved Branson a lot of unnecessary distractions. This week, she was doing the same for Langley. If she decided the call was important, she paged him. If not, she stacked the messages neatly on Branson's desk for either him or Gordon to tackle.

This morning, the array of yellow slips stretched from the middle of the desk to the front. He stifled a yawn and shuffled through them while Gordon started a new pot of coffee. Joshua Kincaid had called just before five yesterday afternoon. He'd located some correspondence from Milton Maccabbe, including several documents with his signature. He was sending them by overnight mail from his office in San Antonio so Langley could compare the signatures with the writing in Danielle's letter.

Buck Bogards had called from the bank. Milton did have a safety-deposit box with them, but he couldn't let anyone open it without a court order. Some more red tape to fill Langley's day, but hopefully the box would contain a legal will so Danielle could go ahead and officially claim the ranch. Otherwise they would have to come up with proof that she was the only living relative. Langley doubted a handwritten letter would suffice for that.

Even better luck would be if there was some reference to the rest of Danielle's family, something that would help her get in touch with her past and maybe inspire the return of her memory.

Gordon tramped back across the room and perched on

the edge of the desk where Langley was sitting. "Coffee should be ready soon."

"Good. I'm sure I'll need it."

"I guess you still have your hands full with that woman who says she's Milton Maccabbe's niece."

"I don't know about having my hands full, but I plan to help her if I can. The evidence indicates she is, in fact, his niece."

"Yeah, I hear her boyfriend's going all around town telling people how you won't let him take her home where he can get medical help for her. He says you have no right to keep him away from her."

Langley leaned back in the chair. "He's probably right. I still have a few questions to ask him, though. I'm hoping he'll volunteer to let you take his fingerprints so we can check them against the ones we found at Milton's cabin the other night."

"Do you want me to be there when you talk to him?"

"I think I can handle it, but I appreciate the offer."

"Well, I know you haven't done this in a while. What did Branson say when he called?"

"The same as you did. He said to dot my *i*'s and cross my *t*'s—make sure I followed procedure."

"Yeah, that's Branson's philosophy, though he doesn't always follow it himself. Not that we usually have much trouble around Kelman."

Branson had also warned Langley that the whole amnesia bit might be a hoax. Samuel and Danielle might be in this together, trying to gain possession of a ranch they had no legal claim to. Only Langley couldn't see Danielle as a con woman. Hopefully, that was intuition and not wishful thinking.

He shuffled through the rest of the messages. Dr. Silvers, the New Orleans psychiatrist who'd treated Danielle, had returned his call. The message said he was relieved to hear that his patient was safe and that he hoped Langley would have Danielle contact him. He left his office number and the number of his cellular phone.

Gordon stretched and stood. "If you don't need anything else from me, I'll mosey on home."

"I think I've got it covered."

"Then I'm outta here. I've had a hard time keeping my eyes open the past couple of hours. These slow nights seem to go on forever." Gordon grabbed his hat and jacket and headed for the door.

"Thanks for the coffee," Langley said as he picked up the phone.

"You bet. Keep your eyes open and watch your back."

Langley only nodded at Gordon's parting comment. He was already punching in the number for Dr. Silvers's cell phone. A minute later, the connection was made.

"Hello." The voice was deep, with a definite New Orleans accent. "How can I help you?"

"I'm the one who left you a message yesterday about Danielle, the amnesia patient who's here in Kelman."

"Langley Randolph."

"Right. I hope I didn't catch you at a bad time," Langley said. "I know it's early."

"No problem. I can't tell you how worried I've been about Danielle."

Langley grabbed a pen from the Dallas Cowboys cup where Branson kept his supply. "She seems in good spirits, considering her situation," he assured the doctor. "What exactly are you afraid might happen to her?"

"It's hard to say with this type of amnesia. I'm fairly confident that eventually she'll remember what happened the night she was attacked."

"Wouldn't that be a good thing?"

"It should be. Except that the actual experience of remembering could be disastrous for her."

"I'm not sure I understand, Doctor."

"My diagnosis was that she was suffering from acute stress syndrome brought on by the assault itself and possibly by what was going on in her life before it happened. I prescribed a tranquilizer, but after the first few days, she refused to take it. I didn't discharge her from the hospital, you know. She just walked out even though I told her it was dangerous for her to be on her own."

Langley twirled the pen. As yet the doctor had said little to help him grasp Danielle's plight. "The danger part is what I'm interested in, Dr. Silvers. In what way do you think Danielle is in danger? Are you talking physically or emotionally?"

"I'm talking emotionally. You'll have to ask the police if you want to know about the likelihood of her being attacked again."

"I've already done that." And he'd gotten a lot straighter answers from them than he was getting from the psychiatrist. "Describe the danger, Doctor. In layman's terms. What might happen to Danielle?"

"All I can do is speculate, based on what I saw of her in the hospital and on the case histories of other amnesia patients."

"All right. Let's speculate."

"I believe she's closed her mind to the assault because it was either too brutal for her to face or because she knows the man who did it to her. Either way, her mind is protecting her from something she's not prepared to face. If and when the memories come rushing in, she may lose control. There have been documented cases where the patient took his or her own life. I'm not saying Danielle would do that, mind you, but it is a concern.''

''She's already had occasions where memories flash through her mind,'' he told the doctor. ''Last night, she heard voices. She became shaky and disoriented.''

''That's not uncommon in this type of situation. But if her reactions become too severe, it could cause a setback in her recovery.''

''So how do I help her?''

''Treat her as normally as possible and don't say or do anything to upset her. If her condition changes or worsens, she should see a psychiatrist. I can recommend someone in your area.''

''If it comes to that, I'll get in touch with you again. In the meantime, I'll see that she's taken care of.''

''And I'd advise you to be careful. She's vulnerable now. She may misread your desire to help, may start reading something more into your actions. If she does, you have to back away. She's a very attractive woman, but she doesn't need any more complications in her life.''

''I'm not planning to take advantage of her, Doctor. If I had been, I wouldn't have called you for advice.''

''Then I hope I've helped.''

Langley wrapped up the conversation as quickly as he could. He longed to discount the doctor's warning about suicide, but he couldn't. He'd been there when the memory of the key and the metal box had sprung into her mind. He'd only glimpsed the shadow of the fear that haunted her, but it had been enough to make his chest grow tight and his stomach settle into a cold, hard ball.

He tossed the pen to the table and walked over to the coffeepot. Possibilities tumbled through his mind as he filled his travel cup with the hot brew. He'd finish returning phone calls from his truck.

He penned a note for Calamity and grabbed his hat. Anticipation quickened his step. He had a burning urge to make sure Danielle was all right, to satisfy himself that she was still coping with the stress of living in the present without the safety net of the past.

He pictured her waking up at the ranch, imagined her hair tumbling wildly about her face, her dark eyes heavy with the residue of sleep.

Damn.

These were exactly the kind of thoughts the doctor had warned him about. He'd have to watch himself with her. He couldn't deny that he was attracted to her. Any man would be. But he could and would keep his feelings in check when he was around her.

For both their sakes.

DANIELLE STEPPED OUT her front door and into the early-morning sunshine. Her first night alone hadn't been as bad as she'd feared, but it had been accompanied by the usual nightmares. Probably the only reason she'd slept at all after Samuel left was the fact that Langley had called to report that one of his hands was riding guard duty. If she had any problems at all, she should yell or else just blink her lights a few times.

Fortunately, she hadn't had to do either of those things. She would, though, if Samuel showed up again. Funny, a few days ago, she'd thought the only thing that could make her feel better would be to have her memory return, to find out who she was and where she belonged.

Now she wasn't even sure she wanted her memory or her past life back. Yesterday, when she'd been soaring above the Running Deer with Langley, she'd felt as if she could take on the world. Last night, listening to Samuel describe what she was like when she lived with him, she'd felt humiliated, almost ashamed.

Stepping over the rotten boards in her rickety steps, she jumped to the ground. She'd gone to sleep last night thinking about the metal box. Langley had agreed it was impossible to search the whole ranch for the mysterious metal box, but she could still look in some of the more obvious places. The bunkhouse fitted that category.

"Good morning."

Anxiety knotted inside her. She turned to see a craggy old cowboy walking in her direction. She took a deep breath and determined to get a grip on her nerves. Surely this was the ranch hand Langley had sent to serve as her bodyguard. She returned his greeting.

"You're up and about early this morning," he said, rubbing his whiskered chin. "You must be Danielle. You're as pretty as Langley said you were."

"Thank you." She extended her hand. He took it in his gnarled one.

"My name's Riff, or at least that's what folks call me. Langley says I'm to keep an eye out for you during the day unless he or Ryder are around." He spit a long stream of brown gunk to the ground. "From the looks of those bruises, I'm probably a little too late."

She studied the man. He was at least sixty and looked as if he'd spent all those years drying in the sun. His skin was a blotchy brown and his face resembled a wrinkled scrap of worn leather. His eyes were the color of murky water.

"Langley says someone's trying to scare you off the ranch," he said, eyeing her suspiciously.

"I'm hoping they've given up."

"If they haven't, I can handle them." He tapped the

fingers of his right hand on the butt of a pistol he wore at his waist. "I brought my welcoming committee with me."

She shuddered at the thought. "I hope you don't have to use that."

"So do I. But I'm not scared to. It's stopped many a snake in the grass, mostly rattlers, but it would do the same for a two-legged snake." He slapped at a mosquito, then wiped his hand on his faded jeans. "Are you going somewhere in particular or are you just out for a morning stroll?"

"I thought I might look around the bunkhouse."

"I don't know why. I doubt it's been used since Milton took over the ranch. He ran this spread all by himself. If he did need a little help with roundup or branding, he just hired somebody to come in for the day."

"I've heard he wasn't very sociable."

"He was downright unfriendly, if you ask me. But you didn't. Tell you what. If you need me, give a holler. I'll be hanging around the house somewhere, close enough to know if anyone comes driving or riding up."

"Thank you, Riff. If I need you, I'll call."

He tipped his hat and headed back toward the corral. She watched him go, then hurried across the spongy carpet of dew-covered grass. The door to the bunkhouse hung at an angle from its rusty hinges, dragging on the ground so it couldn't be fully closed.

She peered through the crack. Light and shadow spawned eerie patterns along the walls and bare wooden floor. Cots strewn with sagging mattresses and frayed Mexican blankets lined one wall. A long metal table had been turned on its side and left leaning against the opposite wall.

And the sickening odor of something rotting away assaulted her nostrils. Her stomach heaved, and she thought she might be sick. When the nausea eased, she pinched her nose with her fingers and stepped inside.

A gossamer spiderweb snagged her hair and eyelids. Cringing, she brushed it away and ran her fingers up the wall. She located the light switch and flipped it up. Nothing happened. The bare bulb that dangled from the ceiling was broken, its jagged edges twisted into the shape of a disapproving frown.

Something moved near her foot, something dark that blended into the shadows. Heart pounding, she bent low enough to make out the hairy form of the tarantula as it crawled onto her tennis shoe. She swung her foot wildly, shaking it until the spider fell to the floor.

She longed to run back into the sunshine, but this might be just the type of place a man like Milton would choose to hide a box he didn't want anyone to find. Stepping cautiously, she moved toward the center of the long, narrow room and peeked into the kitchen. There was a beat-up range and some old iron pots, but the abundance of spiderwebs proved nothing had been cooked in there for many a day.

A bat flew from the rafters. She ducked and then glanced up. Up…and into the face of the woman swinging from the rope knotted around her neck.

The narrow room began to spin around her. The nightmare had returned. Only this time, it was visiting while she was awake.

Chapter Six

Langley knew something was wrong the second he stepped out of his truck at the Running Deer. Danielle was a few yards away from him, walking toward the house in slow motion. Her arms hung limply at her sides, and her gaze was directed straight ahead. If she saw him at all, she gave no indication. The doctor's warning slammed into his brain.

"Danielle." He hurried toward her, only half-expecting her to respond to his call, but she jerked around and stared at him. He reached her side and slowed his pace to match hers. "What happened?"

"Take a look in the bunkhouse." She balled her right hand into a fist and ground it into her left palm. "Someone left me a surprise."

Langley hated the fear and pain that glazed her eyes, but even that was preferable to the stony mask of a few seconds ago. She was coming around now, sliding out of the trance and back into the fiery woman he'd met two nights ago.

"What's in the bunkhouse?"

"A dummy hanging from the rafters. She has long black hair, blood all over her and a knife plunged into her side. Oh, yeah, and purple bruises painted all over her face and arms. Remind you of anyone?''

Langley didn't try to bite back the curses that flew from his lips. ''I want you to go inside and stay there, Danielle.''

She pulled from his grasp and started walking back to the bunkhouse. ''I'm going with you, Langley. I brought these problems here. I need to face them.''

''You've faced enough.''

''I thought that when I walked into the cabin last night and found Samuel waiting for me. Apparently, I was wrong. The real surprise was waiting in the bunkhouse.''

Anger charged through Langley. ''Samuel was here? Riff didn't tell me that.''

''Riff never saw him. He'd come and gone before Riff got here.''

''Damn. Why didn't *you* call me?''

''There was no reason to. He just wanted to talk. It saved me the trouble of going to Gus's to meet with him.''

Langley looked around and spotted Riff working with one of the horses. He waved, then turned his attention back to Danielle. ''What did Samuel want to talk about?''

''Nothing new. He wants me to go back to Fort Worth with him or to let him stay here at the ranch with me.''

''He had no business coming here. We settled that yesterday morning.''

''He thinks he has every right, but we talked awhile and then he left.'' She all but ran the last few feet and entered the bunkhouse before him. She strode determinedly through the rancid living area and into the small kitchen.

Langley only half swallowed a curse. The dummy was

just as she described it. The product of a sick, sick mind. He dropped an arm around her shaking shoulders.

"Why would someone do this? Vandalize the house, hang me in effigy? Beat me to a pulp in New Orleans? As far as I'm concerned, this proves it's the same man who's behind everything. But does he want me dead or just gone?"

"I don't know, but I damn sure intend to find out. And I intend to keep you safe. Inside the law or out."

She reached up and touched the hem of the cotton skirt that had been pinned on the dummy.

"Let's get out of here, Danielle."

"No. Not yet."

She closed her eyes and swayed against him. He took her hands. They were icy cold. "Don't do this to yourself, Danielle. It's not healthy and it's not helping."

She opened her eyes and stared at the dummy. "Those are my clothes, Langley. I've worn that skirt before. I've worn that shirt."

"How can you be sure?"

"I don't remember buying them, but I can see myself wearing them."

He studied the dummy more intently. It was dressed in a sweatshirt with the word "Paris" printed across the front and a long, brown cotton skirt that flared from the waist. Simple clothes, the kind a man might pick up anywhere. Or the kind he might have stolen from Danielle's house or from her luggage, assuming she'd had some with her in New Orleans.

"Those are my clothes," she said again. "I'm as certain of that as I am of anything, which still leaves lots of room for doubt." He led her back outside and into the sunshine. She put her hands up to ward off the glare of the sun. "How long do you think the dummy has been hanging in the bunkhouse?"

"Judging from the lack of spiderwebs on it, I'd say not more than a day or two."

She started walking toward the house. "It's the metal box, Langley. I know it is. I can feel it. Someone wants to get rid of me before I find it."

"If that's the case, that box must hold one hell of a treasure, or at least one that's worth a lot to some lunatic." He wondered if it was also worth a lot to Danielle. If so, the reasons were lost along with her memory.

But those reasons could still get her killed. He had to make sure that didn't happen. He pulled the cell phone from his pocket and dialed his home phone number. First he'd get Ryder to come pick up Danielle and take her to the Burning Pear. It wasn't safe for her to be alone, and his mom would know how to help get her mind off this latest terror she was facing.

Then he'd pay a visit to Arlo Camionos. He'd already talked to Arlo once since Danielle had shown up in Kelman, but he might as well take full advantage of his friend's Texas Ranger training. Arlo had to know a lot more than Langley did about chasing down dangerous criminals within the parameters of the law.

Langley Randolph, acting sheriff. Unwilling lawman. He sure hoped Branson was having a fantastic honeymoon because it might be the last chance he ever had to escape Kelman again. Especially if he expected Langley to pinch-hit for him. Only even if he wasn't filling in for Branson, he'd be hard-pressed not to help Danielle. She'd already burrowed way too deep under his skin.

ARLO WAS OUTSIDE, his head stuck under the hood of his pickup truck when Langley drove up and brought his own truck to a stop. "You got trouble?" Langley asked, lowering his window.

Arlo stopped his tinkering with the engine and looked up. "Not as serious as what you've got."

"So you heard?"

"Ryder called. It's a good thing he did. I was just about to ride out to the west pasture and string some new wire, but it sounds like your problems are a lot more pressing."

"Mine took a turn for the worse this morning. I'm not sure what I'm dealing with, but I know I have to stop it before it goes any further."

"Why don't you come and take a load off while you tell me exactly what you found in Milton's old bunk house? I've got a couple of cups of morning coffee left in the pot."

Langley followed Arlo inside his ranch house. The place fit Arlo. Rugged, no nonsense, straightforward. He'd come back to the family ranch two years ago when he'd taken a bullet in his left hand. The Rangers hadn't wanted to lose him, but Arlo wasn't the kind of man to be happy with a desk job so he'd opted for an early retirement and moved back to Kelman.

Today, Langley was especially glad he had.

Arlo poured the coffee. Langley took one of the crockery mugs and carried it to the kitchen table. "How much did Ryder tell you?"

"Probably as much as he knew, but I'd like to hear your version. You were there. Tell it slow and try not to leave out any details, no matter how minor they may seem."

Langley dropped to one of the wooden chairs and stretched his long legs in front of him. He told the whole story, from finding Danielle in a trance-like state to examining the cruel dummy that had been dressed in what Danielle believed were her clothes. By the time he finished, his muscles had tightened into hard knots and the anger all but consumed him.

He spread his hands on the table, palms down. "I'm open to suggestions. What would you do if you were walking in my boots?"

"It's not the boots you have to watch out for in this case. It's that badge you're carrying. It means you have to play by the rules or get anything you find thrown out of court later."

"I don't plan to let that happen."

"Then I suggest you call the forensics team in San Antonio. They have the equipment and expertise to do this right."

"Do you think they'll take hanging a dummy in a bunkhouse seriously?"

"They will when you tell them about the message that was left in the cabin when it was vandalized and about Danielle being assaulted in New Orleans." Arlo scratched his chin, catching his fingers in his beard. "And especially when you tell them that Danielle believes that the dummy was dressed in her clothes."

"I'd like them to check for prints, see if they match the ones Gordon took from the cabin. The clothes should be tested, too, for hairs or anything else that might tell us who's been in that bunkhouse lately."

"Go all the way with it, Langley. Have them do DNA testing on Danielle's hair. If they find her hairs embedded in the clothes, that will prove her memory flash was accurate and that the clothes really are hers."

Langley took a sip of coffee, but he had no taste for it now. He wanted to make the call to San Antonio and get the show on the road. "One other thing, Arlo. Do you have any connections in Fort Worth?"

"I have connections everywhere in Texas. What do you need?"

"I'd like to take a picture of Danielle and have someone check and see if any of Samuel Drummer's neighbors recognize her. Just in case he's lying about her having lived with him in his apartment."

"I'm starting to worry about you, Langley. You're beginning to talk like a lawman."

"A temporary ailment. Strictly temporary."

Langley thanked Arlo for his help and made a quick exit. It would be a busy day.

"THIS YEAR'S PECAN CROP came in early, but they're a little small. I don't mind the little ones for fudge or cookies, but I like the big ones for my pies." Mary shelled another pecan as she talked and dropped the nut into the bowl she had balanced on her lap.

Danielle stretched her legs and leaned back on her hands. She was in the middle of the living-room floor at the Burning Pear, chatting with Mary and watching Betsy kick her bare feet and play with a soft plastic cow that sported a well-chewed ear.

She knew Mary was trying to take her mind off the morning's events. The amazing thing was that it was almost working. It was hard to imagine anything negative inside these walls. "I appreciate your taking me in this morning. I was more upset than I wanted to admit."

"You had reason to be. It just doesn't make a bit of sense to me. If you hadn't shown up to claim the Running Deer, the place would have gone on the auction block for taxes. So why is someone trying to scare you away?"

"I might know the answer to that question if I could remember anything earlier than two weeks ago. That's what makes this so frustrating." Danielle leaned over and picked up a set of rattling baby keys and jingled them for Betsy's pleasure. The precious baby girl rewarded her efforts with a huge smile and a delightful cooing noise.

"Well, whatever the reason, Langley will find out. You can count on that. I've never seen any of my boys fail to do what they set their minds to. Of course, they sometimes take their own good time at setting their minds to something." She chuckled softly. The sound washed over the room, like cream over hot cobbler.

"How do you do it, Mrs. Randolph? You make me feel like I'm an old friend or part of the family even though you must hate having Langley mixed up with me. I'm nothing but trouble for him."

"If you're asking if I like having Langley out looking for a madman, the answer is no." Mary set the bowl of shelled pecans on the table beside her. "If you're asking if I worry about my sons, the answer is yes."

"I guess I'm asking why you're so quick to open your home to me. You don't know me. I don't even know myself, and so far, even with a last name, we haven't been able to find a record that I exist."

Mary patted the topknot of graying hair on top of her head, then rocked her chair forward, planting her feet on the floor to still it. "I won't lie to you, Danielle. If I had my druthers, Langley would never have met you. He'd never have been pulled into this kind of trouble. And I don't think it's anywhere near over."

"I appreciate your honesty and I don't blame you for feeling that way." And she didn't. It wasn't blame but sadness that tightened around her heart. "I respect your wishes, Mrs. Randolph. I won't come here again."

"Don't even think such a thing. We're way past that. Langley *did* meet you and he wants you here. I don't know what things you've done before you came here or why you've done them. But Langley's my son. Apparently, he sees something in you that's made him want to help you even more than he really has to. I'd trust him if I were you."

"Oh, I do trust him." Danielle jumped up from the floor and perched on the edge of the sofa. Mary must have misunderstood her comments. "I didn't mean to suggest that Langley is anything but a gentleman and totally trustworthy."

"No. I'm sure you didn't. He's the most sensitive of my boys—a lot like his father was." She smoothed her skirt with her work-worn hands. "What I meant was that if Langley sees something good in you, it's probably there."

"I hope you're right."

"Well, I know Langley. He's never brought a woman home to spend the night before. That's reason enough for me to welcome you."

"Thank you, Mrs. Randolph. I feel better already." The words were true. The vote of confidence stilled some of the anxiety that had taken up residence in her heart.

"Then I say we make a big pot of coffee and have a woman-to-woman talk at the kitchen table over a plate of oatmeal cookies." Mary patted her stomach. "Food may not solve all our problems, but it sure makes them more tolerable."

Danielle scooped up Betsy and propped her on her hip for a bouncing ride into the kitchen. A few hours ago, Danielle had stood in the dark bunkhouse, fear and dread so thick she thought she might choke on it. Now she was about to have homemade cookies and coffee in the home of a neighbor.

The contrast was staggering. She wasn't sure if either Langley or his mother were right about the kind of person she was, but at least when she was with them, she felt almost normal.

Betsy wrapped her chubby little arms around Danielle's neck as they stepped into the kitchen. Danielle kissed the top of her head, the soft, wispy hairs like silk against her mouth. She and Betsy were a lot alike. They'd both wound up in good hands even though neither of them knew who they really were or how they'd managed to land in the care of the Randolphs.

As far as Danielle was concerned, it was a miracle.

DANIELLE WAITED all afternoon for Langley to return. The best she got was a phone call just before five. The call was short and to the point. He was going to pick her up at six and take her to the Running Deer to collect her things. For lack of a better way to put it, he was essentially evicting her until further notice.

Only she wasn't ready to leave her uncle's ranch for good, not until she found the metal box or at least remembered what was in it. She feared it was the key to finding out who wanted her dead and why. And if that were true, running away would not solve her problems.

"No." LANGLEY STOOD in the small kitchen at the Running Deer and glared at Danielle. "Absolutely not."

"Aren't you even going to listen to what I have to say?"

"Not on this subject. You are *not* staying at the Running Deer as long as there's a lunatic on the loose around this place."

"It was okay before. What happened to change your mind?"

"My conversation with Dr. Silvers. The stabbed and bloody dummy hanging in the bunkhouse."

"When did you talk to Dr. Silvers?"

"This morning. He's concerned about you."

"That's his job. He's a doctor."

"And it's my job, too, while I'm working for the sheriff."

"I'll be fine, Langley. I wasn't thinking of staying by myself."

"Well, you're sure not staying out here with Samuel Drummer. I haven't ruled him out as a suspect. He had the opportunity. He was on the property." He turned his back on her and stormed into her bedroom. "Get your things, Danielle. You're moving to the Burning Pear."

"Did you check this out with the rest of your family?"

"Why should I? We have plenty of room. Besides, Ryder and Mom are crazy about you."

"I have a better idea."

"Then spit it out, but the answer is no."

"I'll sleep at the Burning Pear, but I want to be here in the daytime."

"So you can play host to a madman? Perhaps you could have him over for coffee. The two of you could chat about why he tried to kill you."

"Just hear me out. All you'd have to do is lend me one of your hands to be my bodyguard. You're doing that anyway."

"One man can't patrol this whole ranch."

"He won't have to. All he has to do is stay with me during the day."

"Why is being here so important to you? You've admitted more than once that you have no intention of living out here permanently."

"I have to be here so I can look for the metal box."

"Be reasonable, Danielle." He leaned against the door frame, his thumbs hooked in the front pockets of his jeans. "You can't search three thousand acres for a small box. You said yourself the only hope of finding it is for your memory to return."

"And that might never happen."

She walked to the window and stared out at the gathering twilight. Langley couldn't see her face, but he could read the slump of her shoulders and sense the turmoil raging inside her. He longed to do something to ease her pain, but he was no good at this type of thing. He was good at running things the way he ran the Burning Pear, but she obviously wasn't accustomed to taking orders.

"You're just upset tonight, Danielle. Not that you don't have every reason to be after what happened this morning, but I'm doing everything I can."

"And I have to do the same." Frustration tore at her voice. She turned to face him, her eyes wet with unshed tears. "I have to do something, Langley, or go crazy. I have to have a past. I have to know who I really am."

"You're Danielle Thibodeaux. And you're alive. That's enough to know for now."

"It's not enough for me. We haven't been able to locate a birth certificate for Danielle Thibodeaux. I have no record of my existence." She trembled and hugged her arms about her chest. "I talked to your mom today, and I ached to remember my own mother. I see you with

Ryder, and I wonder if I have family anywhere who care about me.''

She stepped toward him, and he could read the quiet desperation in her eyes. He opened his arms and she stumbled into them. He held her close, her head tucked under his chin, as her body dissolved into spasms of shuddering sobs.

He tried not to think of the way her hair smelled, all flowery, like a summer day. He tried not to think of the way she felt in his arms, warm, supple. But her gentle curves melded against him, and he could think of nothing else.

This wasn't what she needed, wasn't what he needed. Complications. Attraction so strong it took his breath away. She'd stopped crying, but she still clung to him, and for the life of him, he couldn't make himself let her go.

She tilted her head and met his gaze, and he knew something was happening between them. This wasn't about the argument anymore. It wasn't about going or staying. It was about a man and a woman, and need so real it stripped him of the inhibitions he'd lived with all his life.

He wasn't sure who made the first move, but he knew the second her lips touched his. The kiss was salty sweet, warm, moist. The taste of her consumed him, as if the world had stopped. As if they were the only two people who mattered.

Finally, she pulled away. ''I didn't mean for that to happen.''

''Neither did I, but it certainly felt more right than the other things that have been going on around here.''

''I know.'' She backed out of his arms. ''And I know

my request sounds stupid to you, but it's important to me.''

"I have to admit that I don't fully understand the connection between your finding the box and your getting your memory back, but if being on the ranch to look for the box is that important to you, then we'll do this your way. You can spend your nights at the Burning Pear, and Ryder, I or one of our hands can go with you during the day to search for the box that we're not even certain exists.''

"Thank you. I don't understand it, either, but it's something I have to do. The only family tie I have in my life right now is with an uncle I can't remember. The only thing I know about him is that he wants me to find that box. I have to do that for him. And for me.''

Langley thought about what she'd said while she gathered her few belongings. He wished he knew more about amnesia, but how could he grasp it when Danielle's medical doctor and her psychiatrist hadn't even come up with the same reasons for her inability to remember her past.

But for some reason, she'd become almost fixated on this metal box. A strange legacy Milton had left his niece.

Danielle tucked a paper grocery bag under her arm and slung her backpack over her shoulders. "Okay, cowboy, I think I have everything I need. Actually, I have everything I own.''

"Then let's get out of here.''

She walked to the front door and stopped. "Was it only two nights ago I walked up these steps for the first time?''

"Up the steps and into chaos.''

"Funny, it seems like months ago. But then I guess

when your whole life has been condensed into two weeks of memories, two days is a really long time.''

''Yeah. Only two days with you, Danielle Thibodeaux, is like no two days I've ever known.''

And now he was taking her home to sleep under the same roof as he did. If he thought the days were long, imagine what the nights would be like. This one would definitely start with a cold, cold shower.

IT WAS AFTER MIDNIGHT, but Danielle hadn't slept. The events of the past two days toyed with her mind like a torturous maze that pulled her inside and held her captive, leading her to first one dead end, then another.

And to top it all off, there was Langley, just outside the maze, waiting as if he were the prize for a successful escape. She touched her fingers to her lips and thought of the kiss they'd shared.

Langley Randolph, her protector. Her friend. The only real friend she had in this crazy new world she'd fallen into. But why did she feel this heated attraction to him when her body and mind repelled any contact with the man who claimed to be her lover?

Untangling her feet from the sheets, she slid her legs over the side of the bed. The robe Mary had lent her dangled from the bedpost at the foot of her bed, a flowing length of flowered percale that danced mysteriously beneath the whirling blades of the ceiling fan. Reaching for it, she draped it over her shoulders.

Padding across the wooden floor in her bare feet, she opened the door and stepped into the hall. It seemed strange to traipse through an unfamiliar house in the middle of the night, but she knew the Randolphs wouldn't mind if she stole into the kitchen for a glass of milk to take the edge off her insomnia.

Obviously, she wasn't the only person not sleeping tonight. The aroma of toasting bread and frying bacon wafted on the air, and a blur of soft male voices broke through the quiet. Pulling the robe tighter, she tied it at the waist, fully covering the oversize T-shirt she'd borrowed from Langley.

She stuck her head through the kitchen door. Langley was at the range, turning a strip of sizzling bacon. Ryder was pouring cold milk into two tall glasses.

"Am I interrupting anything?"

They both turned at the sound of her voice. "No," Langley answered, raising the fork in greeting. "Welcome to the party."

"I hope we didn't wake you," Ryder said. "Mom's been at us to tone down our racket ever since Betsy arrived on the scene, but we get started talking and forget all about being quiet."

"You didn't wake me. I haven't been able to sleep. I was just coming down to raid the kitchen myself."

"And your timing is excellent," Langley said. "We're having BLTs on toast. Bacon is one of the few dishes I can actually do a decent job of cooking. Bacon and canned soup."

She was about to tell him she wasn't hungry, but one look at the thick slices of red tomatoes and the bread already layered with melted cheddar, and she changed her mind. "You talked me into it," she said.

"Good," Ryder said. "There's nothing like the company of a beautiful, sexy woman in nightclothes to improve the appetite." He took a third glass from the cupboard and poured more milk.

Danielle maneuvered around the table. "What can I do to help?"

"You can grab the lettuce out of the refrigerator," Ryder said. "I forgot about it."

"Are midnight snacks a ritual around here?" she asked, pulling out a bouquet of leafy red-tipped lettuce.

"No." Langley forked the crispy bacon strips onto a plate lined with paper towels. "But I wasn't sleeping, either, and Ryder was still up watching TV. He's the only night owl among us."

A few minutes later, they were talking and laughing at the table and devouring the food. "The sandwich is wonderful," she said. "Now I can't wait to try your canned soup."

"What you really need to sample is Ashley's chocolate cake. Now that is to die for," Ryder said.

Danielle wiped her mouth with her napkin, catching the toast crumbs. "I'd love to sample your sister-in-law's cake or at least get to meet her. I've heard so many good things about her from Mrs. Randolph. And if your mother-in-law loves you, you must be super."

Langley downed the last of his milk. "You'll get your chance to meet her and all the rest of the family if you're sure you can handle it."

"When?"

"A week from Saturday. There's a festival in town to celebrate harvest. If you're not a rancher around here, you're likely a farmer. Some are both. At any rate, the town goes all out."

"With food," Ryder said. "The way we celebrate everything. All the families bring huge picnic dinners out to the rodeo grounds. There're games and races for the kids, serious horseshoes for the older fellows and a live band for dancing when the sun goes down."

A family affair. Only she wasn't part of this family or any other. She doubted she'd be going to the celebration, but she wasn't about to get into that with Langley or Ryder now.

"It sounds like an exciting night."

"It's a good chance for you to meet your neighbors. And a nice night for me to retire from law enforcement. I talked to Branson today. He's cutting his honeymoon short by a couple of days. He'll be home that Saturday."

Danielle had started stacking the empty plates to carry them to the sink. She stopped short. "He's not coming home early because of me, I hope."

"He offered to come home right away if we needed him. But I don't know what he could do that's not being done already. I've got a friend who's an ex-Texas Ranger and another one who's a state trooper. They give me advice on a daily basis."

Danielle picked up the dishes and deposited them in the sink for rinsing. "Crime in south Texas," she said over the sound of splashing water, "and it seems such a peaceful place once you leave the Running Deer."

The phone rang. The mood in the kitchen changed immediately, as if a cloud of doom had floated over them.

"Who the devil can that be at this time of night?" Ryder asked, but it was Langley who grabbed the receiver.

She turned off the water, her insides quaking as she watched the lines of Langley's rugged, sun-bronzed face twist into tight, angry angles.

"Hold him," he barked into the phone. "But stay put. I'll be right over."

"Trouble in town?" Ryder asked.

"No, it's a lot closer than that. Trouble at the Running Deer."

"I'm going with you," Danielle stated, already heading for the bedroom to jump into her clothes.

Chapter Seven

Langley barreled down the road toward the Running Deer. Danielle fidgeted in the seat beside him, still pulling on the shoes she'd carried in her hands when she'd run out of the house to join him. He'd have preferred her to stay at the Burning Pear, but not only was he in no mood to argue, he also didn't have a leg to stand on. It was her cattle that might be in jeopardy.

He'd instructed Gordon to keep a watch on the Running Deer, but the last person he would have expected to show up in the middle of the night was Joshua Kincaid's foreman. Life was getting more complicated by the minute.

Danielle finger combed her hair. "I don't understand why you're so upset about Wade Hernandez showing up at the ranch. You said that Joshua Kincaid had asked him to oversee the place until it officially changed hands."

"He's there with one of his hands and a cattle-hauling trailer. It's past midnight. Put those two facts together and it sounds more than a tad suspicious to me."

"You think this might be cattle rustling?" She twisted around to face him. "This is exciting. It's just like one of the old Westerns. And I'm riding in with the cavalry."

"Now you find your spirit of adventure." He groaned. "You have strange tastes in entertainment."

"It certainly beats dealing with *my* problems."

"These *are* your problems."

"Then it beats dealing with people trying to kill me and run me off the Running Deer. Unless..." She turned to him. "Unless Wade is the one who wants me off the ranch."

"I don't know if he wants *you* off, but it sure looks like he wants a truckload of your cattle off."

"They're not officially mine yet. And he's surely not stealing them."

"I'll reserve judgment on that until I have more facts."

Danielle scooted to the middle of the seat and laid a hand on his thigh. "Aren't you glad I showed up in Kelman, Texas? Without me, your time as acting sheriff would have been a real bust."

"Yeah," he answered honestly. "I'm real glad you came along to add a little interest to my life. But you can slow it down any time now. I could use some sleep."

DANIELLE LEANED against the kitchen counter and observed the questioning session. Langley sat opposite Wade; Gordon sat opposite the ranch hand whom Wade had brought with him. She'd seen Wade from a distance at the ranch, but he'd never bothered to ride over and introduce himself. He was a lot younger than she'd thought, probably no more than thirty-five. He was tall, muscular, with a scar that ran through his left eyebrow.

He'd answered a few of Langley's questions but not to Langley's satisfaction. Danielle could tell the handsome cowboy was growing more agitated by the minute.

Strange, but even that added to his rugged appeal. She liked Langley a lot, way more than she should, considering the circumstances.

But she felt so alive around him. So normal. And every inch a woman.

Wade pushed his chair back from the kitchen table. The grating sound of wood on Mexican tile grabbed her attention. "I told you, Langley, I just brought the truck over here so we could take some of the stock to auction in Eagle Pass on Friday. Joshua told me to oversee the management of the Running Deer with the same care I do his ranch. That's what I'm doing. I didn't plan to load the cattle tonight."

"And you expect me to buy the story that you do truck deliveries after midnight?"

"I do it whenever I find the time."

"You had a couple of men working over here this afternoon."

"I have men over here every day. The horses have to be fed and watered. Salt licks have to be put out. Fences need repairs. There's always work to do on a ranch. I don't have to tell you that."

"And if bringing over a cattle truck was part of that routine work, there's no reason you shouldn't have done it when the sun was shining."

Wade stood and leaned over the back of his chair, jutting his chin toward Langley. "I'm just doing my job. I'm not looking for trouble, but I know there's plenty going around out here since Danielle Thibodeaux showed up."

"Exactly what do you know, Wade?"

The foreman let his glance walk over her from head to toe before he turned back to Langley. "I know she conveniently can't seem to remember anything about herself except that she's supposed to inherit the Running Deer.''

Anger quickened her pulse, but she bit back the scathing comment that almost flew from the tip of her tongue. She'd let him finish his comments before she jumped into the verbal fray.

''I know she found the place vandalized when she arrived. I know she found some dummy hanging in the bunkhouse and that she got all bent out of shape about it.'' Wade hitched his thumbs into the front pockets of his jeans. ''I know that the talk around town is that her boyfriend came down here from Fort Worth to get her, but that she told him she'd rather stay with you. Evidently, the Randolph money turns her on.''

Langley stood. ''You've said enough, Wade.''

''You asked me what I'd heard. You can't go ballistic on me for telling you.''

Danielle stopped biting her tongue. ''But I can. I want you off my land. You and your men. I'm Milton's niece, and he left the ranch to me. I'll run it.'' She had no idea how she was going to run it, but it would be without Wade's help.

Wade pushed his chair under the table and reached for his hat. ''You'll have to take that up with Joshua Kincaid, Miss Thibodeaux. He's my boss, and I take my orders from *him*.''

Langley stepped into Wade's space and looked him in the eye. Toe-to-toe, Langley clearly had the upper hand even without the authority of the law behind him. His shoulders were broader, his body harder, his manner far more intimidating. ''I'll talk to Kincaid,'' he said. ''You can count on that. But if you show your face on the Running Deer again without Danielle's personal invitation, you'll have to answer to me. Is that clear?''

"Oh, yeah, it's real clear." Wade shoved his hands deep into his front pockets. "Is that all, *sheriff?*"

"As a matter of fact, it isn't. If I find any indication that you have mishandled the financial records for Running Deer or illegally confiscated any of the livestock, I'll advise Danielle to file charges."

"So it looks like Samuel Drummer is right. The Cajun sexpot has you wrapped around her little finger."

Wade and his ranch hand stormed out the door, and probably not a second too soon. The muscles in Langley's arms pushed against the fabric of his shirtsleeves and his hands knotted into tight fists.

"I've never seen Wade like that before," Gordon said. "He's always a little cocky, but he usually don't bite off trouble the way he was gnawing at it tonight."

"Maybe he's not usually cornered."

"I reckon not. You know he's up to no good, sneaking that truck in here at night. Of course, no one would have known it if I hadn't been watching the place. He could have loaded it tomorrow somewhere out of sight of the house and then driven it out of here tomorrow night. Like stealing eggs from a one-legged hen."

Danielle groaned. "And I'm the one-legged hen. Besides which, I have a ranch with no one to take care of it."

"If you hadn't run Wade Hernandez off yourself, I would have." Langley's expression hardened. "I'll call Kincaid tomorrow and tell him he's been relieved of duty. Milton's niece has taken charge of the spread."

She walked over and looked out the window. "All that pasture. All that livestock. I guess I better take a crash course in ranching."

"You can hire some young guys in town," Gordon

said. "They can keep the horses from starving and take care of any emergencies until you hire a real foreman."

"I don't want any new people coming onto the ranch," Langley said. "I'll take over the management and I'll send Riff over to run the day-to-day operations. I know I can trust him." He turned to Danielle. "Unless you have a problem with any of that?"

"No problem."

Langley could run the ranch and the investigation. All she wanted was to find the metal box. And to find herself. After that, she'd sell the ranch and leave all this behind her. And the only thing she'd miss would be Langley.

When the men finished talking, Langley took her arm. "It's late. Let's go home."

"Your place or mine, cowboy?"

"Well, mine has a bed."

Gordon looked at them from the corner of his eye.

She shook her head. "We're teasing, Gordon."

"I knew that."

DANIELLE SAT IN the porch swing that Riff had installed for her and studied the names and facts she'd pulled up in her genealogical search on the Randolphs' computer. More dead ends. Milton Maccabbe was apparently as much a nonentity as Danielle Thibodeaux.

She'd been in Kelman, Texas, five days now. She'd gone shopping for boots and appropriate ranch wear and spent hours exploring the property. But she was no closer to finding the metal box, a will or anything about her past. The only good news in all of this was that neither Wade Hernandez nor Samuel Drummer had returned to the ranch though Samuel still called her every day and she'd had dinner with him at Gus's once and met him for coffee twice.

His irritation grew more obvious with every encounter. She could understand his frustration. He was the person she should be turning to, but she was never at ease around him. The more he wanted from her, the stronger her urge to pull away from him.

He blamed the alienation of her affection on Langley, but in truth it was Samuel's attitude that made her keep her distance. He wanted too much from her, wanted her to jump back into the relationship he said they'd had. But she couldn't remember ever being with him, and when he tried to hold her hand or even put his arm around her shoulders, she felt as if the air was being forced from her lungs.

Other than the growing tension that existed between Samuel and her, things were going almost too smoothly. When the next shoe dropped, it would probably be a steel-toed size twelve. Maybe it would take that to spur her memories to the forefront of her mind. She still experienced the sporadic, sometimes almost traumatic, flashes of the past, but the bits and pieces never fitted together in a way that made sense. A box, something about a creek, a well, an accident. A puzzle whose edges had been sliced away so that no clear picture emerged.

But oddly enough, in spite of the persisting amnesia, she still retained skills and basic knowledge. Recipes, songs, poems, computer skills, even TV personalities came in loud and clear. And all the while, her name, her age, where she went to school, the town she'd grown up in, her parents—everything that really mattered—was lost.

She'd talked to Dr. Silvers several times on the phone and he'd assured her that this was "normal" for an amnesia patient, that not remembering the name or the face of her fiancé was to be expected.

But he'd cautioned that, in her fragile condition, she might emotionally attach herself to another male if one was available and helpful. He'd been right. She had. Her attraction to Langley grew stronger every time she was near him even though Langley seemed determined to avoid a repeat of the kiss that had knocked her socks off the other night. The protective rancher was the bright spot in her days even when he brought bad news the way he was probably on his way to deliver right now.

But good news or bad, she couldn't wait to see him.

LANGLEY CRAWLED OUT of his truck and took the steps to the Maccabbe cabin two at a time. Danielle was in the porch swing, her dark hair falling around her shoulders, her lips parted in a smile. As usual, his heart sped up at the sight of her. As usual, he tried to ignore the fact. She was another man's fiancée even if she didn't remember the man.

"Good news," he said, stopping a few feet from her. "Or at least partially good."

"That beats the competition by 110 percent. Hit me with it."

"The first round of DNA testing came back. They were able to match the hair samples you gave them with some of the hairs on the sweatshirt."

"So my flashback was accurate. The clothes were mine. Which means either the man stole them from me when he attacked me in New Orleans or else he took them from the apartment in Fort Worth. Did they find any hairs that didn't belong to me?"

"A few."

"What's the next step?"

"I'm going to see if Samuel will voluntarily donate a few hair samples for testing."

"Let me ask him. I think he'll be more receptive if the request comes from me."

"Without a doubt. He's convinced I'm trying to railroad him. But that's not the only news. The court order came through. I was finally able to pick up the contents of your uncle's safety-deposit box." He dropped the brown envelope onto her lap.

"Did you find a will?"

"No, but I found a birth certificate."

"Milton's?"

"No. This one was George Lackland's."

"Who's that?" She pulled the sheaf of papers from the envelope.

"I'm not sure. He appears to be about the same age as Milton. He was born in Mansfield, Louisiana. I looked the town up on the map. It's in the northwest corner of the state, just a few miles from Shreveport."

"Why would he have that man's birth certificate in his safety-deposit box and not his own?" she asked.

"I don't know. I was hoping the name Lackland meant something to you."

"No. Maybe we can locate him, but I don't know how that would help unless George Lackland is a close friend of Milton and might know where I lived."

"I've already run a make on George Lackland. He died in South America thirty-five years ago."

"George Lackland was that easy to track and yet we can find nothing on Milton Maccabbe's past, not even the name of his parents. That doesn't make sense."

"It does if George and Milton were the same person."

She massaged the muscles in the back of her neck. "Why would Milton change his name?"

"He didn't legally. He may have taken a false identity. There are any number of reasons why a person does that. But it usually boils down to the same basic cause. They don't want to be found by someone."

"That might also explain why he was such a loner. A person who doesn't want to be found would keep a low profile."

"Exactly."

She thumbed through the rest of the stack of papers. It was mostly records for equipment and horses he'd purchased.

Langley moved her printouts out of the way and sat down beside her so he could read over her shoulder. "There's a deed to the ranch in there, near the bottom of the stack. Milton owned it free and clear. As his only living relative, it will pass to you. Once we establish for certain that you are his only living relative."

"I'd still feel better if I had an actual will. I'd hate to sell the place and then find it wasn't mine to sell."

"You don't have to sell. You could stay here and live on the ranch."

She looked up and met his gaze, and the awareness that always hovered between them intensified. His chest tightened. He wanted to kiss her so badly he could taste it. If he stayed there another minute with her looking at him like that, he would. But a kiss would never be enough to satisfy him.

He stood and tugged his hat a bit lower on his head. "I'm going to take a look at the horses and the saddle inventory. I'd like to see if what's on hand matches up with the receipts that were in the safety-deposit box."

"Give me a minute to grab my hat and I'll go with you."

He had the distinct feeling that she knew he was running away from her and that she'd still chosen to follow. If she had, she was treading on dangerous ground. A man could only take so much temptation.

LANGLEY CAME OUT OF the tack room to find Danielle standing motionless in front of a tall sorrel with a flowing mane and a white blaze that ran from his ears to his mouth. The horse tapped his foot as if begging for attention. She reached up and scratched his face. "So you want to be friends. I'd like that, too." She looked at Langley. "Do you know his name?"

"I don't have a clue."

"In that case, I'll call him Lancelot. He's big and quite proud. And very handsome for a horse."

"I thought you weren't interested in anything without seat belts," he said, walking over to join her.

She shook her head and rubbed a spot just below her right temple. "I know it sounds odd coming at this late date, but I think I know how to ride. The saddles, the reins, the harnesses, the bridles. I know about them."

"When did you discover that?"

"A few minutes ago. I had another flashback, only this one didn't upset me. Actually, it felt warm, almost like a hug. I was a little girl, about nine or so, and I was with my grandpa." She ran her fingers through her hair. "We were both laughing and he was teaching me to ride."

"Did you catch a name?"

She closed her eyes for a second, then opened them. "I hate the way this happens. I never remember enough. He called me Danny, but all I called him was Grandpa." She nuzzled the sorrel. "I'd like to ride someday soon."

"How about now? It's time you see your land from the back of a horse."

"*My* land. Only I can't set foot on it without having someone beside me." Frustration tugged at her voice.

"It won't be like that forever. The man who's tormenting you will be behind bars one day soon and you'll be able come and go as you please."

He ached to take her in his arms and comfort her, but even that action would backfire on him. He had to keep her at arm's length. It was the only way to keep the attraction between them from heating to the boiling point.

He nudged his hat back on his head. "I'll let Riff know I'm taking over his bodyguard duties for a while. I'll saddle up Lancelot for you and the big roan for me. Riff had them both out for a run yesterday. He said they were surefooted and handled the saddle well."

"Okay, but give me a few pointers in case my memory's playing tricks on me and I really don't know a thing once I climb into the saddle."

"I will, but you're smart. Even if you haven't ridden before, you'll catch on fast. If you run into trouble, I'll be right beside you all the way."

"Then I can't possibly go wrong."

THE SKY WAS BRIGHT BLUE and cloudless, and the south Texas wind blew cool and steady as they started across the brushy grassland. Langley knew at once that Danielle was an experienced rider. She was relaxed in the saddle, swaying with the movement as if she was an extension of the spirited animal beneath her.

She held him to a walk at first. Langley matched his speed with hers, giving her time to soak in the sensation of riding again. "How does it feel so far?"

"Wonderful. Freer than I've felt since—just free and alive!"

She avoided mentioning the attack and resulting amnesia, but Langley knew exactly what she meant. He also understood her reluctance to bring it up and let the memories of it intrude on her excitement.

"Let's go faster," she said. "I want to feel the wind in my face."

"Lead the way."

She gave her mount some rein, taking him to a canter and then a gallop. Her hair flew behind her, the thick black curls bouncing off her neck and shoulders. Turning, she called back to him. Her voice tinkled like a schoolgirl's, and he could feel his need for her clear down to his toes.

She slowed as she neared Branson Creek, and he caught up with her.

"This is a good place to dismount for a while," he said, reining in his horse. "A spring feeds the creek, and a lot of wildlife water here in late afternoon."

"Does the creek have a name?"

"Branson Creek." He held her reins and gave her a hand while she climbed from the saddle. "It runs across our property, as well."

"I remember seeing it from the helicopter. Was it named for your brother?"

"No, for my grandfather. Branson Wilson Randolph. He settled the ranch originally. My dad increased the acreage considerably after they struck oil. There are still some operating wells in the northwest quadrant of the ranch. Dillon handles that aspect of the land. I'm the cattleman, and I like it like that."

Langley led the horses to the creek for a drink of the cool water. Danielle walked at his side. He squatted and picked up a small rock from the water's edge. Choosing a target on the other side of the creek, he skipped the stone across the glassy surface of the water.

Danielle used a leafy twig to smooth a spot between the exposed roots of an oak tree. She sat, hugging her knees. "Thanks for riding out here with me, Langley. You were right. Seeing the ranch from atop a horse is a very different experience."

"Was it more exciting than seeing it from a helicopter?"

"I'd have to think about that." She raked her fingers through her hair, but the action did little to tame the windblown tresses. "I'd have to say those two experiences have been right at the top on my excitement chart." She dug her heels into the dirt. "Right below our kiss."

Langley dropped the stone he had just picked up, his self-control suddenly as shaky as the legs of a newborn calf. "I had no right to kiss you."

"Because I'm engaged to a man I don't even know?"

He considered his answer. She deserved the truth—if he could figure out what that was. "I don't want to add complications to your life, Danielle."

"When the pail is running over, another drop of water isn't going to matter. Besides, I never think of you as a complication."

"Dr. Silvers thinks I could be."

"Dr. Silvers doesn't know me. I'm just one of his very rare amnesia patients." She unclasped her hands and picked up a stick. Resting her chin on her knees, she drew a heart in the dirt. "Have you been in love before?"

He didn't have a clue where that had come from. The question made him uncomfortable. *Not* having been in love at his age made him seem like some kind of freak.

He searched for an evasive answer. "I dated the same girl all through college."

"That's not what I asked."

"Then I guess the only honest answer is no. I tried to convince myself I was. I even asked her to marry me. Fortunately, she was smart enough to turn me down. I broke out in a cold sweat from pure relief."

Their laughter was quick and easy, and just as quickly fell to silence. Danielle dropped her stick and rubbed her hands on the legs of her jeans.

"I date occasionally," Langley admitted. "But to tell you the truth, I don't think much about love anymore. If it happens, it'll take me by surprise." The way his attraction for her had.

Danielle doodled with her stick, making wavy lines in the dirt. "I've thought about love a lot the past few days." She stretched her legs in front of her, destroying the heart she'd drawn in the dirt. "I don't know if I was ever in love before, but I don't think I could have been in love with Samuel Drummer."

Langley walked over and leaned against the tree. "He says you were."

"I know. But nothing clicks when I'm with him, at least nothing pleasant. Nothing stirs my blood or warms my heart. Nothing like…" She looked up and met Langley's gaze. "I never feel with him the way I feel when I'm with you."

Desire swept through Langley, a surge so powerful he had to brace himself to control it. "We can't do this, Danielle. You're in my care and you're engaged to another—"

She stood and cut off his protests with her fingers on his lips. "Don't you ever quit being perfect? Don't you ever just let yourself feel?'' She rose on tiptoe and touched her lips to his.

Her kiss was wanton, deliciously aggressive and yet sweet and giving all at once. The restraint he'd held on to so diligently evaporated in the searing heat that claimed his body. The hunger took over and he kissed her like he'd never kissed any woman before.

Finally, she pulled away, but he couldn't. He buried his lips in the heated flesh at the base of her neck, then trailed a path back to her kiss-swollen lips. The pager at his waist vibrated, but he hardly felt it. The movement was nothing compared to the throbbing of his own body.

Groaning, he pulled away and checked the number. It was Riff, calling from Milton's cabin. ''Time out,'' he whispered, ''but don't go away.''

''No, I couldn't. I'm too weak to move.''

Langley yanked the cell phone from the pouch at his waist and punched in the number. He listened while Riff gave him the details and watched while Danielle soothed the telltale wrinkles from the front of her blouse.

''So tell me, what's the latest catastrophe?'' she asked when he broke the connection.

''How do you know it's a catastrophe?''

''Let's just say I'll bet you're a lousy poker player.''

''One of the worst.'' He took her hands in his. ''Riff says you have company.''

She moaned. ''Not Samuel. Please, don't let it be Samuel right now.''

''It's not, but you may not like this caller any better. Another of Milton's mystery relatives has just arrived at the Running Deer to claim the ranch. And this one claims he has a will.''

Chapter Eight

Riff spit a stream of tobacco over the side rail of the porch as Langley and Danielle approached the cabin. "Ain't this something? A man dies and all of a sudden relatives come out of the woodwork."

"Where is he?" Langley asked.

"He's inside. Probably marking his territory. No offense to you, Miss Danielle, but it's still amazing to me how when you're dead and gone, everyone claims kin to ye."

"No offense taken, Riff." She climbed the steps and stopped to hear what else the aging ranch hand had to say before she and Langley went inside to meet the newest Maccabbe relative. Riff was cantankerous, but he always said exactly what he was thinking. Of all the Randolph hands that she'd met, he was her favorite, and, according to Langley, he was the most dependable when you needed a job done right.

Riff rubbed the whiskers on his chin with his characteristic deliberation. "The man's mighty uppity, just marched in here like he already owned the place."

Langley stepped to the door and grabbed the knob. "So let's go inside and meet—what did you say his name was?"

"Corky Westmorland. Only Wants-more-land would probably be closer to the truth. He says Milton was married to his mom back in the eighties. Humph. Can't you just picture some woman putting up with Milton Maccabbe?"

"You notice she's not still around." Langley swung open the door and held it for Danielle. "What about you, Riff? Are you coming in?"

"Nope. I've got work to do, but I wouldn't go believing anything this man has to say unless he's got proof. He looks like a snake-oil salesman to me and I don't call many a man wrong."

"I've never known you to," Langley agreed. "I'll be cautious."

Danielle heard Langley's footsteps behind her as she walked into the kitchen she'd come to think of as hers. Corky Westmorland sat at the table, thumbing through a copy of *Texas Monthly* and stuffing himself on the peanut butter cookies she'd baked that morning.

"Make yourself at home," she said, not bothering to hide her irritation that he'd done just that. Still, she wasn't going to let Riff's snap judgment influence her. Corky might be just the missing informational link they were searching for.

Corky glanced up, then flipped the magazine shut. He cracked a grin and showed a set of perfect white teeth as he looked her over with a little too much enthusiasm.

Langley took care of the introductions, explaining that he was filling in for the sheriff. He behaved in his usual professional but friendly manner though she could tell he was sizing Corky up. When he finished, he got right down to business.

"Riff tells me you have a will stating that Milton left his ranch to you."

"I sure do. I got it in the mail a few weeks ago, with a letter from Milton saying he had cancer and didn't have much longer to live. I thought I'd come down here and check it out, but the old guy outside said Milton had already died."

"About three weeks ago." Langley took the chair opposite Corky. "Were you in touch with Milton before he sent you the will?"

"No, that's the real kicker. I hadn't heard from him in years. I was only fourteen when he and my mom split up, and I figured he'd forgotten I existed."

"Do you mind if I see the will?"

"You can look at it. I'm not turning it over to you, though. Not that I don't trust you, but I've got to watch out for my own interests." He pulled the folded will out of his shirt pocket and pushed it across the table to Langley. "I'm planning to contact a lawyer tomorrow. Do you know who Milton used?"

"No one that I know of."

Corky turned to Danielle. "The old man who was here a minute ago said you're living here now. If I'd known old Milton had friends like you, I would have come calling on him years ago."

She walked over and took one of the remaining chairs at the table. "I'm not Milton's friend. I'm his niece."

Corky showed his pearly whites again. "You're kidding, right? My mom said Milton didn't have any kin. She said that was his best quality. Actually, I think she might have said *only* good quality."

Langley refolded the will but didn't hand it back to Corky. "Danielle's not kidding. She's his niece and she has a letter stating that her uncle was leaving the Running Deer to her."

Corky's eyebrows arched and his mouth twisted like

a corkscrew. "I don't understand. He can't leave the place to both of us, can he?"

"He could, but that's not what either your will or Danielle's letter says."

"So what does this mean?"

"It looks like a case for a judge to decide."

Corky's voice rose and his Adam's apple jumped up and down. "I don't have money for a court battle. I have a will, and it looks legal to me."

Langley put up his hands. "You might as well save that for an attorney."

"Well, what do I do in the meantime? I have my suitcase in the car, but I can't afford to put up in a hotel for weeks while we settle this thing. I was planning on staying right here on the ranch."

"*That* you can't do," Langley said, tapping one end of the folded will against the table.

"You mean because Danielle's staying here. I have an official will. You said yourself she only has a letter." He turned back to Danielle. "I'm not trying to kick you out. Hey, you can stay here with me. I like company."

The gleam in his eye finished his statement. Definitely a snake-oil salesman, she decided, although she'd never heard that particular term before, at least not that she remembered.

"So how about it, Danielle? I'd love to have you stay out here with me. Who knows, we might hit it off real well."

"Sorry, I don't come with the land."

"Too bad."

Langley walked over to stand behind Danielle's chair. "If and when the Running Deer is officially granted to you, you can kick Danielle out and move in yourself. Until then, she's a blood relative and she's following the advice mailed to her by Milton just before he died. Written by Milton's own hand. Which means the ranch is off-limits to you unless she invites you onto the property.''

''A pretty little niece who has the local law in the palm of her hand. I get the picture.''

Danielle's blood boiled. The man was a pompous jerk. Still, he had a will. What kind of cruel joke had her uncle planned during his last few weeks of life?

Langley propped a booted foot on the back rung of her chair. ''I don't think you do get the picture, so I'm going to help you a little with it before I escort you out the door. I don't know what Milton had in mind when he sent you that will. I don't even know for certain that he was the one who sent or signed it. There are no witnesses and it's not notarized, so I'm not even sure it's official.''

''Like you said, that's for a judge to decide, not you.''

''Right. But I'm investigating some criminal activity that's been taking place around the ranch. As long as I'm involved, no one else is moving onto the property to complicate things. That includes you unless I get a ruling that says you are the legal owner. That's the picture you need to get.''

Corky let out a low whistle. ''Crime in this little country town? Nothing serious, I hope.''

''Serious enough, and everyone with ties to the Running Deer is a suspect. That would include you, now that you've shown up with a will.''

''You can investigate me all you want. I'm as clean as the Monday-morning wash.'' He shook his head and pushed the stack of uneaten cookies at his fingertips to the middle of the table. ''And you can have this place for now, Danielle, if you're crazy enough to hang around in the middle of a cow pasture with some criminal running around the place. Me, I'm outta here.''

Langley and Corky kept talking a little longer. Danielle stepped away as Corky's words rolled through her mind.

Corky didn't want to hang out in this isolated area with a criminal, but that was exactly what she was doing. Searching acres of cow pasture for a metal box that she was certain her uncle wanted her to find.

Perhaps Corky had a lot more sense than she did. He was leaving the Running Deer. And she was staying. The perpetrator, as Langley called their suspect, was probably staying, as well. And he could be anyone. Anyone at all.

Even Corky Westmorland.

"OKAY, RYDER, ABOUT one inch to the left.''

He complied, and Danielle took a few steps backward in order to get a better look as Ryder stretched to position the painting over the fireplace. She'd painted the walls in the living room yesterday, a shade of pale green that softened the Sheetrock and covered greasy handprints.

Now Ryder was helping her hang some pictures Mary Randolph had rescued from the attic at the Burning Pear. She wasn't sure why she was bothering except that she had to keep busy or go crazy, and the place was a lot more inviting now that she'd fixed it up.

"How's this?'' Ryder asked, repositioning the picture.

"Perfect.''

Ryder drove in the nail, then slipped the picture wire over it. He backed up to stand beside her. "You've really done a lot with this place. If Milton were here, he wouldn't recognize his old cabin.''

"Yes, only now I may have to give it up even sooner than I expected."

"I wouldn't worry about that yet. Langley thinks the will Corky Westmorland has is a fake. I'd have to agree with him. Milton isn't the type to go to the trouble of writing an official-looking will. And if a lawyer had done it, his name, or at least the name of the firm, would have been on the letterhead. And he would have had witnesses attest to Milton's signature."

"Still, Corky has that official-looking will, which is more than I have. But if the will is authentic, I can't understand why Milton would have sent me the letter saying he was leaving the ranch to me if he had already willed the Running Deer to Corky."

"Langley's still trying to track down a record of the marriage between Milton and Corky's mother. It may not exist. Add that to the fact that no one around here knows about an ex-wife or a stepson, and Corky's story equals scam in my book."

"You never heard of a niece, either, until I arrived in Kelman." Danielle straightened the picture. "A metal box, a will, a letter and a key. I try to think kindly of the dead, but it's getting harder every day. I feel like I've been drawn into some twisted game that Milton devised as he was dying. Do you suppose he's perched on a cloud somewhere laughing at all of this?"

"Milton Maccabbe perched on a cloud?" Ryder smiled broadly. "Now that's a sight I can't imagine."

"No one seems to think too highly of my uncle except Joshua Kincaid."

"I wouldn't put a lot of stock in his assessment. Kincaid is known for having some pretty unsavory characters in his hire."

"Your mom never speaks badly of Mr. Kincaid."

"My mom never speaks badly of anyone. Besides, Joshua and my dad grew up together, so their friendship goes way back. Mom thinks if my dad liked the man, he can't be all bad."

"But you disagree."

"Let's just say I have my doubts that the man's business dealings are all legitimate. He owns Kincaid's. That's a string of Texas-theme nightclubs that stretch across the state. Dillon is convinced that his customers pay to do more than two-step and ride mechanical bulls."

"Such as?"

"Bookmaking. You know Texans."

"Actually, I don't, although I'm learning fast."

"Well, they like their sports events and there's always a few who will bet on pretty much anything if you'll give them halfway decent odds. It's all illegal. No taxes paid, of course. And a lot of people end up over their heads in debt. Others, the ones who run the gambling operations, end up with millions stashed in foreign banks. Dillon is determined to find out if that's the case with Kincaid."

"Senator Dillon Randolph must be a strong opponent of illegal gambling."

"Dillon's a strong opponent of anything that's illegal or bad for the state of Texas. He's a family man, and he wants his son to grow up in a world that's getting better, not worse." Ryder laid the hammer on the mantel and bent to rub his knee.

Danielle stepped back to admire the effect of the painting on her new green wall. But it was Ryder who drew most of her attention. "Dillon chose politics, Branson chose upholding the law, Langley chose ranching, while you chose the rodeo. You're a very versatile and talented family."

"Yeah, we're alike in more ways than we're different, though. I'll give up riding broncs for good one day and marry and raise a family. When I do, I'll settle into ranching, at least some phase of it. No one can compete forever. It's a life for the young and physically healthy." He propped a booted foot on the hearth. "Being a little crazy helps, too."

"When do you think your knee will heal enough to let you start competing again?"

"Maybe as early as next season."

He walked over and dropped to the sofa, another piece of furniture provided by the Randolphs. Mary had insisted it was just sitting in one of the back bedrooms gathering dust, and she'd had Riff and one of the other hands deliver it to the Running Deer. She wanted to make sure Danielle had a place to rest during the day, just in case she was still weak from her injuries.

Danielle couldn't imagine any woman being more thoughtful or loving than Mary. No wonder her four boys had grown into such caring, responsible men.

Ryder clasped his hands behind his neck and leaned back. "I'll be able to compete again soon, but it may take me a while to get to the top again."

"How did you have that accident? You said you weren't bronc riding at the time."

His eyes shadowed, as if he had drifted into an unhappier time. "I'd met a lady friend of mine for lunch. We'd finished eating and she was crossing the street to get in her car and go back to work. She worked for Joshua Kincaid, believe it or not."

"It's a small world."

"Yeah. She'd been distracted during lunch, upset

about a friend she worked with who had just up and quit his job. Anyway, she was crossing the street and this car rounded the corner going ninety to nothing. I don't think Kathi even saw it. I shouted and jumped into the street to shove her out of the way."

"Oh, no. And the car must have hit you instead."

He nodded. "I almost managed to dodge it, but not quite. The impact threw me against a parked car. I was lucky to escape with nothing worse than a busted knee."

"Your friend Kathi must have been extremely impressed by your heroic act. And grateful."

"I couldn't say."

Danielle fought back a shudder as she watched Ryder's face take on a hardness that made him seem years older.

"I never saw her again," he said, his voice reflecting his loss. "She had me fooled. I thought we shared something special, but she was just another buckle bunny."

"A what?"

"A rodeo groupie. They hang around as long you're winning. When you're down, they move on."

"Did you try to get in touch with her?"

"No. I figured if she didn't care enough to visit me in the hospital, I didn't need her. I came back home to the Burning Pear and I've been there ever since, trying to find the same thrill in working cattle that Langley does. So far it hasn't happened."

"Langley's one of a kind."

"So you've noticed."

"I've noticed." She sensed the heat rise to her cheeks. She couldn't explain the attraction she felt for Langley, but she knew it had something to do with the strength of him. Not in the muscular sense, though he was certainly well endowed in that department. But it was his strength of will and character that stirred her soul. It was the way she felt when she was with him—excited and yet unafraid.

Most of all, it was the way she felt when they kissed.

If the situation were different, if she had anything to offer besides a past that was suspect at best and the fact that someone wanted her dead, she'd use every feminine wile she had to go after the rugged rancher who turned her insides to mush.

As it was, she'd have to face Samuel Drummer again soon and try to imagine that she had ever experienced that same passion with him. She'd have to talk to him and listen to his stories of what it had been like between them, striving desperately to find some word or image that would trigger memories and open the door to her past. A lifetime locked away in the dark vault of amnesia.

Her past. An uncle whose background was murky. A man who'd tried to kill her and now was trying to frighten her off the ranch. A fiancé she dreaded spending time with. But she should know soon enough if he was the one who'd attacked her in New Orleans and put the dummy in the bunkhouse. He'd willingly donated a few strands of hair for DNA testing and even offered to take a lie detector test. He insisted he had nothing to hide.

"You look upset," Ryder said. "Is there something I can do for you?"

"Yes. You could get me away from here for a while."

"At your service. Where would you like to go?"

"Anywhere there are people leading normal lives."

"I know just the place. I'll take you shopping. You can buy a new dress. I hear that's always good for a woman's soul."

She stared at her faded jeans and bleached T-shirt. "I guess I do look a little threadbare."

"I'm not complaining about the way you look. I'm just trying to cheer you up."

"Shall I take a young steer with us to use for bartering purposes?" she joked.

"Only if you have very expensive tastes in dresses."

"I guess we'll find out. Another experiment into discovering the likes and dislikes of Danielle Thibodeaux."

RYDER TRIED TO MAINTAIN a stream of carefree chatter as they drove into town, but his mind wouldn't cooperate.

Kathi Sable. Everything he'd told Danielle about her had been true, but it was the things he'd left unsaid that haunted his dreams and ran roughshod over his heart.

The teasing lilt to her voice, the sexy swing to her walk, her enthusiasm for life. The way they'd made love. Even now, after all these months, he sometimes woke up at night with the taste of her on his lips.

"Is something wrong, Ryder? You look a million miles away."

The sound of Danielle's voice jerked him back to reality. "No. I was just thinking about someone."

"Anyone I know?"

"Not even anyone I know. I only thought I did." He forced a smile as he turned back to Danielle. "Now let's talk about this dress you plan to buy."

DANIELLE STOOD IN FRONT OF the full-length mirror in the dressing room of Griffith's Department Store, awed by the transformation. She'd stepped through the door a lady rancher, but it was a sexy seductress who smiled back at her from the dressing-room mirror. The red dress hugged her bodice and waist and then flared out in layers of fabric to swirl about her thighs, the hem riding the flesh just above her knees.

Debbie Griffith stepped behind her and fastened the snap at the back of the neck. "It looks great on you."

"Do women actually dress like this in Kelman?"

"Sure they do. Those who can. Not many women do that much for a size six."

Danielle put her hand to the plunging neckline. "It seems a little low."

"My motto is if you've got it, flaunt it. Of course, I haven't had it in years, but when I did, I sure flaunted it. Not all the time, mind you, but often enough that Bill popped the question and has been hanging around smiling ever since." Debbie winked. "Bill still talks about one dress I had when we were dating. I was slimmer then, of course. It was black and backless and hugged my body as if it were painted on. It's not a bad image to leave in a guy's mind."

"I agree, but where would I wear this? Certainly not for ranching."

"It's a simple dress, Danielle. It's your figure and good looks that make it dynamite. You could wear that dress anywhere. It would be perfect for Harvest Night. You'd knock Langley Randolph right off his feet."

Danielle stared at Debbie's reflection in the mirror, her excitement over the dress lost in her dismay at the woman's observation. Talk like that would not be good for her or for Langley. "There's nothing between Langley and me. Our relationship is purely professional."

"I'm sorry. I must have gotten the wrong impression from what I've heard."

"What did you hear?"

Debbie shrugged her shoulders. "You know how it is in a small town. People talk."

"Well, they shouldn't. It's not fair to Langley. He'd treat anyone else in my position with the same professional courtesy. That's the kind of man he is."

"I know what kind of man Langley Randolph is, Danielle. Everyone around Kelman does. He's honest and hardworking, and he'd give anybody the shirt off his back if he thought the person needed it. But he's still a man. And you're a woman." Debbie bent and straightened a spot where the hem had turned up. "And if a spark exists between the two of you, that's just the way it is."

A spark? It was more like a four-alarm fire. Only she didn't know what to do with it and she wasn't sure that Langley did, either. It seemed wrong to want one man when she was engaged to another, even if she didn't remember him.

But far more important was the issue of her past. She had no right to become involved with Langley when she had no idea who she really was or what kind of life she'd led.

"I didn't mean to upset you, Danielle. None of this is any of my business. I guess Bill and I are so happy I just want everyone else to be, too. Now why don't you step into the store and get Ryder's opinion on the dress?"

Danielle turned for a side view. "I guess it wouldn't hurt to get another opinion." The skirt swished around her thighs as she walked out of the dressing room. Her heart skipped a beat. It wasn't Ryder but Langley who was waiting for her to appear. And the look on his face told her exactly what he thought of the sexy red dress.

LANGLEY STOOD SPEECHLESS. The femme fatale in front of him was not the rancher lady he'd left that morning. Her long black hair was gathered on top of her head and tied with a satiny ribbon that cascaded down her slender neck. The soft cotton fabric of her dress draped low in front, revealing smooth ivory cleavage.

"Do you like it?" She whirled around for him to get a back view.

He swallowed hard. "Like would be putting it a little mildly."

"Good," she said, her voice breathy. "Woman cannot live in jeans alone, or at least that's what Debbie says."

"Well, you clean up real good." He struggled to keep the moment light while he fought the crazy urge to take her in his arms and kiss her. That would really set the gossip wheels in motion and give Samuel even more ammunition to hurl against him. "I vote you buy the dress. It would be a shame to leave it hanging on the rack when it looks that good on you."

"You talked me into it." She started heading to the dressing room, then turned back to face him. "How did you know I was here?" she asked. "Did Ryder call you?"

"Actually, I called him."

"Is something wrong?"

And as always, there was. "I just got Samuel's DNA report. None of the hairs on the clothes we found on the dummy were his."

She grimaced, then forced a smile. "In a way, I'm relieved. It was tough believing I might have been engaged to a man who tried to kill me."

"Don't rule out that possibility yet. This doesn't prove it wasn't him. It just doesn't prove that it was. The bad part is we're parked at another dead end."

"So much for buying a dress to lighten my spirits."

He watched her walk away, the sight of her cracking his self-control. Dillon had warned him on the phone that afternoon that he'd be foolhardy to get too attached to a woman he knew nothing about. Dr. Silvers had warned him that Danielle didn't need any more complications in her life. But Langley knew he was already in way over his head and falling deeper by the minute.

He'd just have to deal with it. His job was to make sure she stayed alive and healthy. And to take her home to more bad news.

DANIELLE HELD ON TO her plastic-encased dress as Langley opened the door to her cabin. The sofa in the living room looked familiar. So did the picture on the wall. "One day I'm going to step inside and not recognize this place," he said, "or else I'll just think I'm back at the Burning Pear."

"Your mother keeps sending things over. I'm beginning to feel like an annex."

"I'm sure you're making Mom very happy. She likes nothing better than being neighborly, unless it's spoiling Betsy or Dillon's son, Petey."

"She still finds time to spoil her adult sons, too, I notice."

"I can't complain, at least not about my treatment at home." He stepped over to the sofa. "I do have some complaints about the way the investigation is going, though."

She hooked the hanger of her dress over the door that led to the kitchen. She groaned. "Sit down and I'll pour us a glass of lemonade before you lay the complaints on me. I made a fresh pitcher this afternoon before I went shopping.'' She turned and walked into the kitchen.

Langley had just dropped to the sofa when he heard her scream, a terrifying sound that ripped his heart right out of him.

Chapter Nine

Langley raced across the living room. Adrenaline pumping and heart pounding, he hit the kitchen door, then stopped cold at the sight.

Blood dripped from Danielle's hand, but she probably hadn't noticed. She was deathly pale, stamping as if performing some wild dance and brushing a half-dozen huge, hairy tarantulas from her face and jeans.

He grabbed a clean dish towel and held it gingerly against her wound, exerting pressure above it to slow the loss of blood. "You're okay, baby, you're okay. They look ferocious, but they're not poisonous."

He tried to keep his voice steady though agitation raged inside him. That many spiders didn't turn up by accident.

"What happened?" he asked when she'd quit fighting the spiders.

"The lemonade." Her voice was high-pitched and shaky. She shuddered again as a spider fell from her hair. "I'd covered the pitcher in aluminum foil, but when I took the cover off, it wasn't lemonade anymore. Just spiders." Her voice faded to a whisper.

Langley tackled the countless possibilities jelling in

his mind. "The dirty coward must have broken into the cabin while you were out shopping."

She sucked in a shaky breath. "It's not going to stop until I leave here, is it?"

And probably not then, but Langley held his tongue. Danielle didn't need any more terror in her life right now. He lessened the pressure. The bleeding had slowed but hadn't stopped entirely.

"We have to take you to the clinic and get stitches. You were lucky the cut didn't go any deeper than it did."

She looked at her hand as if seeing the cut for the first time. "How did I do that?"

"You must have thrown the pitcher against the counter when you saw the spiders. Then my guess is you just slammed your hand into a piece of the jagged glass while you were knocking the spiders away."

"The spiders are all I remember. They were crawling out of the pitcher, jumping onto my arms and my clothes." She looked around the room. "Where are they now?"

"The unlucky ones are stamped to smithereens and back. The rest of them scurried under the baseboards, gone to tell their cousins about their narrow escape from the wild woman."

She smiled, and the poignancy of it split his heart in two. No matter what happened to her, she always came back fighting. And whatever the blow, she never lost that magical softness that broke through his defenses and melted his resolve not to let her know how she affected him. He held her so close he could feel the racing of her heart and hated the madman all the more.

"There's a bottle of peroxide under the kitchen sink," she said, pulling away from him and examining the cut.

"The first-aid supplies were some of the few items not destroyed when the human tornado struck."

"I'll get it." Langley stooped and rummaged for the dark brown bottle while Danielle held her hand under the faucet and washed it beneath a stream of cool water.

"It smarts like crazy. I can't believe I didn't notice right away that I'd cut myself on the broken glass."

"The tarantulas had all your attention."

She shuddered again and groaned. "I'm glad their bite is not as bad as their appearance." She held out her arm and hand toward Langley and winced as the peroxide bubbled into the cut, the excess running off into the sink. "Do you really think it needs stitches? The bleeding's almost stopped."

He nodded. "It needs stitches. You don't want to run around a ranch with a gaping wound in your hand. That's just asking for trouble."

"And why should I do that? Since trouble comes calling so frequently now, maybe I should rent it a room."

"At least you still have your sense of humor."

"Put that on my tombstone."

Langley grabbed his jacket and draped it over her shoulders. Her sense of humor was far more intact than his. He was not about to joke about tombstones. Especially not Danielle's.

GUS LEANED AGAINST the counter in his corner café and watched the two strange bedfellows munching on burgers and cracking jokes at one of his back tables. Corky Westmorland and Samuel Drummer. Both strangers to Kelman, and both about as welcome as hornets in an outhouse.

He wasn't eavesdropping, at least no more than he usually did when business was slow, but he couldn't help noticing that every time he came near, they stopped talking. The only things they were vocal about were their feelings toward Langley. He supposed that mutual aggravation was what had bought them together. That and the fact they were both strangers in a small town that didn't get too many strangers.

He picked up the coffeepot and walked over to offer refills. "Can I get you fellows anything else?" he asked, adding more hot brew to their cups. "I got some great pecan pie. You can have it à la mode."

"None for me," Samuel said. "I'm going back to the hotel and make a phone call to my fiancée. She counts on my good-night calls."

"I'll take you up on it," Corky said. "I haven't had any pecan pie in a long time. I'll have a double dip of vanilla ice cream on top."

Samuel scooted his chair back from the table. "You'll never get into shape eating all that food."

Corky patted the spare tire around his waist. "Well, maybe I'll go on a diet when I move out to the Running Deer. Right now, I've got nothing better to do in this town than eat."

Gus went back to the counter and dished up a piece of pie with a couple of scoops of ice cream. He watched out of the corner of his eye as Samuel laid some wrinkled bills on the table, then headed to the front door. He gave a wave as the bell over the door signaled his departure.

Gus carried the pie to Corky. "So you're Milton Maccabbe's stepson. None of us knew he'd ever been married."

"Sounds to me like a lot of people around Kelman didn't know about him."

"You saying you knew him better?"

"My mom did. Enough to know he was bad news. She just didn't find it out soon enough."

"He was a loner, but he didn't cause any trouble," Gus said, for some reason feeling the need to defend the man though he'd never really liked him. "He never hurt anyone."

"So you say. I don't imagine the folks he put six feet under would agree with you."

"If you're saying what I think you're saying, that's a pretty strong accusation."

"Well, he's dead, so I don't guess he'll come gunning for me."

Gus felt the flesh prickle on the back of his neck. He'd served Milton a few times in this very café, but he'd never suspected that he might be feeding hamburgers and lunch specials to a killer.

He still had his doubts, but you just never could tell with a man like Milton. He never talked of his past and never buddied up to anyone in town. He just took care of business and kept to himself. He might have killed a man back somewhere in his past.

"Where's your momma now?" Gus asked. "Did she marry again?"

"She died a few years ago, but she never married again. My dad and Milton were enough to cure her of believing in love."

"Did she ever hear from Milton?"

"Not one word after the divorce. I was twelve at the time they married and fourteen when she told me we were leaving Florida, just the two of us. That's the last time I saw Milton, so you can imagine my surprise when I opened the manilla envelope and pulled out a will saying he was leaving me his ranch."

The bell over the door clanged again and the Griffiths

strolled in, laughing and talking, the way they always were. Still in love after thirty years of marriage. Not like Milton and Corky Westmorland's mom.

A nervous energy propelled Gus as he walked over to greet his new customers. He was dying to pass on what he'd learned to Langley. He didn't know if it would help in figuring out if Corky had anything to do with Danielle's troubles, but it was mighty interesting all the same.

DANIELLE CLIMBED FROM the shower at the Burning Pear. Part of her had wanted to go back to her uncle's cabin tonight and confront the terror that was stalking her. She longed to stand in the front door and scream for whoever was behind it all to step out from the shadows and face her. She was tired of running, tired of waiting for the next blow to strike.

The hardest part of all was not knowing if the man was determined to drive her away from the Running Deer or to simply drive her mad. Now she wasn't even sure about the metal box. It had seemed so real the other night, but nothing seemed that real anymore. The nightmares and reality had become so enmeshed that it was difficult to tell them apart.

Using her uninjured hand, she rubbed the thirsty terry towel over her wet body. A few hours ago, she'd dressed in the silky red dress. She'd felt sexy and provocative, practically like a siren. And then Langley had appeared. Desire had flamed in his eyes, and she'd wanted to crawl into his arms and assure him that the amnesia had stolen away her memories but not her ability to experience the emotions he aroused in her. She didn't fully understand the mystifying attraction that colored their every encounter, but she couldn't deny it.

She didn't want to deny it. She wanted to be a normal woman with normal sensual urges. She wanted to like a man who liked her back, one who didn't survive on a cache of memories she didn't share with him. Grabbing a fresh towel, she wrapped it around her hair, turban-style. She'd comb out the tangles in the guest room.

The floorboards of the old house creaked as she padded down the hallway, the flowered robe falling loosely about her shoulders. The walls were bathed in darkness except for the glimmer of silvery moonlight that peeked around and through whispery curtains.

A soft cry wafted up the staircase. Danielle stopped and listened until she heard the sound again. It was more of a whimper than a cry, but it signaled that Betsy was waking up. More often than not, Betsy slept through the night, but occasionally she woke up hungry or wet and demanding attention.

Danielle scurried down the stairs, her unbandaged hand brushing the smooth wood of the banister. If she was quick enough, she could reach Betsy before her soft cries turned to howls and she woke up the rest of the household.

Pushing through the nursery door, she stopped, her breath catching as she realized that someone else was already in the room. In the darkness, she could barely make out the tall, male frame. "Langley?"

"Yeah." He flicked on the night-light. "I was trying to persuade Betsy to go back to sleep, but she seems to think it's playtime."

Danielle stared at Langley, mesmerized by the sight of his long legs beneath a pair of hip-hugging gym shorts. He was shirtless, and wiry blond hairs sprinkled his bronzed broad chest and muscled stomach. A rugged male with a baby girl in his arms. The image took her breath away and made her suddenly aware that she was naked beneath the thin robe.

She crossed the room, managing to steady her breathing and get somewhat of a grip on her lustful thoughts as she did. A good thing because now that the light was on, Betsy was convinced she'd won the battle. She let loose a string of ga-gas and tried to squirm from Langley's arms to the floor.

"Oh, no, you don't, little princess. Your old uncle isn't that much of a pushover. If I put you down to play, you'll be up for hours." He changed his grip and she stuck her pudgy hands into his face, pushing and grabbing at his nose.

"Do you think she's hungry?" Danielle asked. "Or maybe she needs a dry diaper."

"I think the little conniver just woke up and decided she'd like company, but a bottle might settle her down so we can get some sleep. I was hoping I could keep her quiet enough so you wouldn't hear her."

"I had the same thought. Only you beat me to the nursery."

"I didn't have as far to come."

"You get the bottle and I'll change her," Danielle offered, holding out her hands to Betsy. The wide-awake youngster did a nosedive in her direction. Danielle grabbed the squirming baby and balanced her on her hip.

"You're the patient," Langley said. "I'm supposed to be taking care of you."

"You did. Now I'm stitched, bandaged and ready for action." A blush heated her cheeks as she thought about just what kind of action she'd been thinking of a minute ago.

Long before Langley returned with the bottle, she'd

managed to change Betsy's diaper and button the footed jammies back over her kicking legs.

"You are a little cutie pie, aren't you?" she cooed. "You know you have a houseful of cowboys at your beck and call. And why not? You're so precious. Yes, you are."

Danielle settled in the nursery rocker. Reaching over, she flicked off the night-light and started singing a lullaby. Betsy squirmed at first, then quieted. Apparently, the song worked.

"Vous chantez en français."

She looked up. Langley leaned against the door frame, watching her. "What did you say?"

"You were singing in French. At least that's what I meant to say."

"I was, wasn't I? I hadn't realized it. A French lullaby. My Cajun heritage sneaking through amnesia's barriers, I guess."

"It was very pretty."

"Merci." She looked down at Betsy. Her eyelids had grown heavy, but she was fighting not to give in to the pull of sleep.

Langley handed her the baby bottle and she nudged the tiny pink lips with the nipple. Betsy kept her mouth shut tight. Her eyes flickered open for a moment and then she let them close.

"I don't think she's hungry," Danielle said. "I'll rock her for a little longer, though, before I try to put her down."

"Well, if I can't interest Betsy in warm milk, how about you? I could make some hot chocolate."

"With marshmallows?"

"Big gooey ones."

"Then you're on."

Danielle watched him walk away. She knew he was afraid to get involved with her, afraid that when her past came bursting forth into her mind, she'd rush back to the life she'd lived before the attack.

The fear was real. But her past still lay beyond her reach. Her mind was riddled with abysmal holes that her memories used to fill. But her heart was full of Langley Randolph. Part-time lawman. Full-time cowboy. All man.

DANIELLE WAS IN the guest-room bed, propped up on a mound of fluffy pillows, her feet and legs tucked under the covers. Langley was in the chair that sat beneath the double windows, his bare feet propped on the wooden chest at the foot of the bed that held extra blankets and warm knitted throws. He had decided she deserved to have her hot chocolate served in bed after the events of the night.

Danielle nursed the steamy mug. "I hate to bring up the subject, but tonight when I went for lemonade and found tarantulas instead, you were about to deliver a bit of bad news."

"Are you sure you're up to it? It could wait until morning."

"Why wait? I'm sure there'll be a new supply of problems tomorrow."

"Touché. It's just that I've done some more checking on Samuel Drummer's story. My friend Arlo had a Fort Worth policeman talk to his neighbors. The cop showed them your picture. Only one of them had ever seen you."

"Only one. Probably because I was too temperamental and moody to step outside the apartment."

"That's another part of his story that lacks credibility.

I haven't seen you isolating yourself inside the cabin since you've been in Kelman even though you have plenty of good reasons to hide.''

"How does he explain the fact that only one of his neighbors has ever seen me?''

"He says that the others are lying. They just don't want to get involved in trouble and that they wouldn't talk to the police on general principles. The sad thing is he could be right about that. Officers of the law get a bad rap in lots of places these days.''

"But having one neighbor who recognizes me means Samuel is probably telling the truth about my living with him.''

"Maybe. But even that neighbor wasn't able to give us any additional information about you.''

"Is there any good news?''

"A dab. I had all of Milton's phone records checked.''

"Did you find anything?''

"Only one number wasn't local. He'd called a lawyer in Eagle Pass the week before he died. I talked to the lawyer by phone. He said that Milton had called him and asked him a few questions about writing a will. He answered as best he could without knowing all the facts but suggested Milton come in.''

"Did he?''

"No. In typical Milton fashion, he said he'd already learned what he needed to know.''

"He may have been getting that information for the will he sent to Corky.''

"Not if Corky told us the truth about when he received the will. The phone call was made later.''

"So he may have written a will and left the ranch to

me after we'd talked on the phone, after he'd told me about the metal box.''

"The dreaded metal box." Frustration lined Langley's face with deep grooves. "I wish I was as convinced as you are that the box holds the answers to the mystery of who tried to kill you and why."

"I'm not even all that convinced myself anymore, but I can't give up on it. It's all I have to go on. I'm only thankful there have been no more attempts on my life. I'm hoping that means whoever wants to get rid of me has abandoned that idea."

"More likely it means our culprit hasn't had the opportunity to try anything. You haven't been left alone in days."

Danielle ran her finger around the rim of her cup. "So that's why you think he's resorted to spiders?"

"For now."

"Then I hate to think what new terror he's cooking up." She shuddered as a chill settled around her heart. "Let's talk about something more pleasant." She sipped the hot chocolate, grateful for the warmth.

"You pick the topic," Langley said. "I'm not sure I know any pleasant ones anymore."

"There's always Betsy. I'm constantly amazed that you and Ryder handle her so well. You're really fond of the little darling, aren't you?"

"Yeah, we all are. It will be tough if and when we have to give her up, but she should be with her real parents. Branson is still doing what he can to find them."

"I keep forgetting she's not really a Randolph."

"So does my mom."

"She looks like a Randolph." Danielle took another sip of the chocolate, parting her lips to sample the gooey marshmallow floating on top. "I was noticing the picture of her hanging in the hall. It's hard to tell her baby picture from the ones of you and your brothers. She has the same nose and big ears.''

''Big ears? That's the last time you get your midnight cocoa served in bed.''

''Not big now. You caught up. But they look kind of big in the baby pictures.'' She patted the side of the bed next to her. ''Come sit over here and tell me the details of how Betsy ended up at the Burning Pear.''

''It's not the prettiest of bedtime stories.''

''I'd still like to hear it.''

Langley stepped across the floor and dropped to the bed beside her. ''We were celebrating Mom's birthday. The whole family was here. We're big on birthdays around the Burning Pear.''

''Somehow I knew you would be. I can't imagine your mother missing a chance to have her family all together. She's so excited about Harvest Night she can hardly talk of anything else.''

Langley set his empty cup on the bedside table. ''That night was no exception. Everyone was laughing and talking at once. We had just cut into the cake when we heard a knock at the door. Branson went to answer it, and the next thing any of us knew, we had a woman bleeding from a gunshot wound lying in the foyer. Just before she passed out, she handed Betsy to my mother and told her that the infant was named Betsy and that she was her granddaughter.''

Danielle struggled to form the image in her mind. ''Did you know the woman?''

''No. My brothers and I had never laid eyes on her before that night. Branson took her to the hospital, but before she regained consciousness, or at least before she let anyone know that she had, she slipped out of the hospital and disappeared.''

"Why would she do that?"

"She was afraid. At any rate, by that time, Branson had tracked down her sister, Lacy.''

"Wait. Isn't Lacy his wife's name?"

"One and the same. That's how they met. So I guess you'd have to say Betsy brought them together in a roundabout sort of way.''

"But where did Lacy's sister get Betsy? Or is her sister still missing?"

"No, Kate showed up eventually. It was actually Lacy the gunman was after all along. Kate had just gotten caught up in the danger, but that's another story, for another night. The bottom line is that Kate's boyfriend called her at work and told her that he had a baby who'd been fathered by one of the Randolphs of Kelman, Texas, and he wanted her to help him collect a ransom.''

"So Betsy had been kidnapped. How frightening.''

"That's what Kate thought. She rushed home. Her boyfriend wasn't there, but the baby was. She wanted no part of the kidnapping, so she grabbed the baby and rushed over here with her. On the way, she was forced off the road and shot. She walked through the woods to get here, and then passed out from loss of blood just inside our door.''

"She was lucky she made it. I don't know how she kept from getting lost.''

"It was night. She probably followed the lights." He raked his fingers through his short blond hair and stretched the muscles in his neck and shoulders. "So now you know the rest of the story.''

"How did you get to keep Betsy with your family?

Don't they have agencies that take over when a child's real family can't be located?''

"Mom is very persuasive. You should know that by now. She convinced the Family Services social worker that she should be allowed to care for Betsy until her real family was found.''

"Lucky for Betsy. If I had a child and couldn't be there to take care of her myself, I'd want to know she was in the hands of the Randolphs.''

"If you have a child and you can't take care of her, or him, bring him over. I'll teach him to brand.''

He turned and touched the tip of her nose with his finger. She knew he meant the touch to be casual, only he didn't pull his finger away. He trailed it to her lips and outlined them with sensuous strokes that left her weak with wanting.

"And now I better get out of here and let you get some sleep.'' His voice was husky, his breath shallow.

She reached over and took his hand, curling her fingers between his. "I have a better idea.''

"I was afraid of that.''

"Lie down beside me, Langley.''

"I want to.'' He met her gaze, and she saw the desire burning in his eyes. But he let go of her hand and turned away. "I'm not sure I've ever wanted anything more in my life.''

"Then what's stopping you?''

He slid from the side of the bed and stood staring down at her. "You. Me. The way I feel at this moment. If I lie down beside you, I'll never be able to walk out on my own without making love to you.''

Anticipation washed through her, hot and wet, so

strong she could taste it. She rose to her knees and wrapped her arms around his neck. "Lie down beside—" Her words were lost, swallowed up in Langley's kiss as he climbed back into her bed.

Chapter Ten

The house was quiet except for the pounding of Langley's heart. He had told himself over and over all the reasons why he shouldn't make love to Danielle, but right now, he couldn't remember a one of them. He couldn't think at all, not with her mouth on his. His body was going crazy with a hunger that robbed him of control and scared him to death.

She wanted him. He wanted her, wanted her so desperately that just her kiss seared into his very soul. He couldn't understand his feelings for her. They had come on so fast and so strong, so different from anything he'd experienced before. All he knew was that if he had to walk away without making love to her, he thought his very heart might explode.

He stretched beside her on the bed. She feathered his mouth with kisses, teasing pecks she punctuated with quick movements of her tongue. He captured her mouth again and they sank into a deep kiss that left them both gasping for air.

She trailed a finger down his chest, poking it under the waistband of his gym shorts. "You have too many clothes on," she murmured.

"You want it all, don't you?"

"Right on, cowboy. It's time something went my way."

He tugged on the belt of her robe. It flared open. He wasn't sure what he expected, but one glimpse of her naked body and his insides caught fire. He struggled for a steadying breath as he lay mesmerized by the smooth ivory flesh of her perfect breasts, the nipples pink and pebbled. He let his gaze fall to her tiny waist, to the curves of her hips, the taut stomach and beyond.

"You take my breath away, Danielle."

"I'm glad. I want you to want every inch of me." She took his hand and pressed it against her breast. "This is like the first time for me, Langley. It's all I remember of making love. I want it to be perfect. I want it to be beautiful. Most of all, I want it to be with you."

"I couldn't bear thinking it would be with anyone else."

"Nor could I." Her voice caught on the words.

Desire surged through his veins mingling with another emotion, one that tightened around his chest like a binding of silk. Painful, yet warm and seductive. He started to pull her close, but hesitated when his arm brushed the bandage on her hand. He leaned away from her, balancing himself on his elbow. "I don't want to hurt you."

"Don't worry, I'm watching out for the wound. If you hurt me, I'll let you know."

"All this activity could make it start bleeding again."

"I'm fine, Langley." She trailed his shoulder with wet kisses. "And you still have too many clothes on. I want to feel you against me. All of you."

"Who am I to argue with a beautiful naked lady?" He felt her gaze as he peeled the gym shorts from his aroused body. She ran her fingers along the inside of his thighs and he swallowed a moan. ''You make a man glad he's a man,'' he whispered, finding her lips again.

''I'm only glad you're you.''

''Oh, Danielle. I've tried not to want you like this, but every second we're together I want you more.''

''I feel the same. At another time in our lives, we could have drowned in slow, wet kisses for days before taking it further. But life is too precious now to waste. And tomorrow is too unsure.''

''Don't talk like that. Nothing is going to happen to you. I won't let it.''

''Just make love to me, Langley. Make me crazy, the way you're doing now.'' She touched her lips to his chest and then worked her way down his abdomen, each kiss searing a path that was driving him over the edge.

He tried to return the favor, wanted her to savor the thrill that she was giving him. He turned her onto her back and explored her exquisite body with his fingers and lips. Each time she writhed in pleasure, his own insides quaked, until the need raging inside him approached mind-numbing torture.

''I'd like to make this last forever, Danielle, but I can't. I'm crazy with wanting you.''

''I know. Me, too.'' She touched him and guided him to her.

He felt the strength of her legs as they wrapped around him, burned with the heat from both their bodies as he entered her.

''I can't believe I've ever felt this way before,'' she whispered. ''It's too new, too wonderful.''

''Too perfect.'' He longed to make the moment last, but he couldn't hold back. He thrust deep inside her, over and over, the blood rushing from his head and leaving him crazed with emotions he didn't understand and didn't want to control.

"I love you, Langley. I probably shouldn't, but I do."

Her words took him over the edge. He exploded inside her, his heart pounding so hard and so fast he thought it might never return to normal again. He knew he'd never be the same.

Tiny moans still escaped her lips as she melded her spent body against his. They lay quietly, their bodies slick and warm and entangled. Finally, she stirred beside him.

"I almost wish that the amnesia would last forever, Langley, that there was no past besides us."

"Don't think about that tonight. No pasts. No problems. Just this moment."

"Okay." She touched her lips to his neck. "But I want you to know that no matter what the future brings, I'll never be sorry we had tonight. Never. No matter what happens between us. No matter what happens to me."

"I'll call you when you celebrate your eightieth birthday and see if you still feel that way," he teased, trying to keep her from retreating into the terror that a madman had brought into her life. A madman and her uncle.

She punched him playfully and ran her toes down his bare calves.

All of a sudden, he was springing to life again. "I hope you haven't planned on getting a lot of sleep tonight," he said, nuzzling his face against her breasts.

"I'd sure be disappointed if we did."

Langley planned to make sure she wasn't disappointed.

DANIELLE WALKED THROUGH the cabin the next morning, the delicious ache in her thighs reminding her how lucky she'd been the night she walked into Gus's Corner Café and into the care of Langley Randolph.

Only a week ago, and yet last night when she made love with Langley, she'd felt as if she'd known him forever. Everything about being with him had seemed so right. She loved the gentleness of him, the way he kissed, the way he made her laugh. The way he brought every part of her body to life.

And every time she thought about what it was like to make love with Langley, she was more certain than ever that she had never done that with Samuel Drummer.

She'd been thinking about what Langley had told her last night, how only one of Samuel's neighbors recognized her picture. Samuel could have concocted the whole story about her being his fiancée so he could get her off the ranch or else stay there with her.

Only Samuel had called again this morning, begging her to let him come out and visit. She'd turned him down. But he'd seemed so disappointed she'd spent the rest of the morning wallowing in guilt.

She hadn't planned for it to happen this way. She'd never intended to hurt Samuel. She'd never expected to fall in love with Langley, but she had.

Dr. Silvers would deny it was real. So would Samuel, but she knew what she felt.

The sad thing was that she had no time to revel in the thrill of being in love. The danger was too real. Hopefully, there really was something on the ranch that Milton wanted her to find, something hidden in a metal box. She'd heard the words so clearly she had to believe they were an actual part of her memories. Either that or she was nuts, and she wasn't ready to accept that possibility.

Only what could be in the box that would make someone commit such desperate acts? Money? Most likely. Greed was extremely powerful. But if it was money, why hadn't Milton just put it in a bank?

Unless it was money he wasn't supposed to have. Stolen money. Money he'd made illegally. The walls of the small cabin started closing in around her. She headed to the door and wide-open spaces.

The ringing of the phone stopped her. She picked up the receiver. "Hello."

"Hello, Danielle. This is Joshua Kincaid. I'm glad I caught you at the cabin, but if I missed you there, I was going to try the Burning Pear. I understand you've been spending a lot of time there."

"The Randolphs have been very helpful."

"I'm sure they have been. Mary Randolph's the salt of the earth. And I'd feel much more remiss about not taking better care of Milton's niece if I didn't know you were in such good hands. I'm just sorry about our little misunderstanding. Wade told me everything. He was very upset."

"I appreciate your taking care of the ranch before I got here, Mr. Kincaid, but—"

"Please, call me Joshua."

"Okay, Joshua. I'm sure you were a good friend to Milton, but Langley Randolph's taking care of the ranch now. If you have any questions about what happened the other night, it would be better if you take them up with him."

"Why don't I talk to you? It's your ranch, or at least it will be if your claim of kinship is validated or a will is located. Besides, I have a proposition you might be interested in."

"What kind of proposition?"

"Look, it's so hard to talk business over the phone,

and I've wanted to meet you anyway. Among other things, I'd like to pay my condolences for the loss of your uncle. This would be the perfect opportunity for us to get together. I could be there in a couple of hours.''

''Are you in town?''

''Yes, I just drove in from the San Antonio airport. I always try to make it back for the Harvest Night celebration. That way, I can see all my old friends and neighbors at once.''

Danielle tried to think of a good reason to say no, but there really wasn't one. Joshua had apparently been a good friend to her uncle, and he'd certainly gone out of his way to see that Milton's cattle had been cared for, even if Langley did suspect that Wade had used the situation for his own financial gain.

''Okay, Mr. Kincaid. I'll expect you, and I'm looking forward to talking to you about my uncle. You seem to be the only person who knew him well.''

''Thanks, Danielle. I look forward to meeting you, too, and I think you'll like what I have to tell you.''

They said their goodbyes and she hung up the phone. She was finally going to meet the infamous Joshua Kincaid face-to-face. If he were half as fascinating as his reputation, the meeting wouldn't be dull. And he might be able to give her insight as to why her uncle had been so secretive about the fact that he was leaving her the ranch. If Milton had been in trouble or involved in something illegal, Joshua Kincaid might be the only one who knew about it.

She picked up the phone and punched in the number Langley had given her.

''Sheriff's office.''

''Hi, Calamity. This is Danielle. Is Langley around?''

"He's in the office talking to a couple of guys from the FBI. I can get him for you if it's important."

"Probably not as important as a meeting with the FBI. Just give him a message for me."

"Fire away."

"Tell him that Joshua Kincaid is dropping by the Running Deer in a couple of hours. He says he has a proposition for me. I think Langley might like to be around when Mr. Kincaid comes calling."

"So, the big guy is paying you a visit. Watch him, he's a charmer. Good-looking, too."

"Is that so? Langley never mentioned that."

"He wouldn't. You have to call on me for that type of information." They both laughed.

After hanging up, Danielle grabbed her hat. She couldn't imagine why the FBI had turned up at the Kelman sheriff's office. Still, if there was any way Langley could be at the ranch when Mr. Kincaid arrived, she was sure he would. The distrust between the Randolph men and Joshua Kincaid was low-key, apparently never flaring into open confrontation, but it ran very deep. She'd picked up on it from the first time Langley had said the man's name.

Danielle pushed open the front door and stepped into the sunshine. Riff was hauling a stack of lumber up the rickety steps. He grinned when he saw her, then leaned over and spit out a stream of tobacco. On anyone else, the habit would have been repulsive. On Riff, it seemed as natural as the unkempt graying hair and the grease-stained shirt.

"What's the wood for?"

"The steps. Not that they need repairing," he joked. "But the wood in them's older than dirt. I'll fix that porch railing, too, afore somebody leans in the wrong spot and goes headfirst into that thorny hedge.''

''I'd probably be that someone.''

''I expect you'd be fine. You're not much bigger than a bar of soap after wash day, but I doubt it would take the weight of a full-grown man.''

''All the same, I won't lean until you have it fixed. Can I get you anything? Water? Iced tea?''

''No, I've got a big thermos of drinking water in the back of my truck. I came prepared and ready for work.''

''Then I don't suppose I could persuade you to take a ride with me. I'm getting cabin fever sitting inside.''

''Are you talking about riding horseback or just bouncing around the ranch in my truck?''

''I thought we could take a couple of the horses out. I rode Lancelot the other day.''

''Lancelot?''

''That's what I named the sorrel. It seemed to fit him.''

''Nothing like a horseback ride over an open range to make you forget your troubles. This porch-fixing can wait.''

''Thank you, Riff.''

''No need to thank me. I don't ever need to be asked twice to put down a hammer and ride the range.''

A few minutes later, they'd saddled the horses and headed out toward Branson Creek. A gust of wind whipped her hair into her face. She brushed it away and nudged her hat back a little farther on her head so she could get a better look at the sky. The sun was still bright, but a thin veil of gray clouds was rolling in from the west, and she could hear the low rumble of thunder off in the distance.

She'd already learned that clouds and distant thunder

in south Texas seldom meant rain, but still they probably shouldn't go too far. Besides, she'd have to get back in time for her meeting with Joshua Kincaid. Lancelot reared his head. He was ready to gallop. She gave him more rein and let him have his way. Riff followed along behind her.

Funny, there was a world of problems she should be thinking about, but riding into the wind with the sun on her back, all she could think of was last night. And Langley.

When they reached the creek bed, she slowed Lancelot to a walk. A group of white-tailed deer stepped into the open. They watched her and Riff for a second, their big brown eyes staring to see if the intruders were friend or enemy. Then one turned and darted back into a cluster of mesquite, and the rest followed.

"I don't know how you keep from getting lost out here," she said when Riff rode up beside her. "Acres of brush, sparse grass and cacti, all crisscrossed by a maze of barbed wire and fence posts. And all of it looks pretty much the same."

"Not once you get to know it. On a clear day like this, you use the position of the sun. But there's other landmarks, too, things anyone can follow."

"You mean like the creek or one of the windmills?"

"Yep. Or the old Simpson place. Look over to your left. You'll see the chimney poking right up over that cluster of mesquite. It's due west of the cabin. Find the chimney and you can find your way home."

"Can we ride over there?"

"We can go wherever you like. You're the boss lady."

The boss lady. Now that had a nice ring to it. She headed Lancelot in the direction of the old Simpson home. They'd almost reached it when a sharp whistle brought her to a halt. She turned to find Riff waving at her to stop. Circling, she guided Lancelot back to where Riff was dismounting. Just beyond him was a section of fence that had been knocked to the ground.

Riff walked over and propped a booted foot on one of the fallen posts. "Looks like this fence got a little help in collapsing."

"You don't think someone knocked it over on purpose, do you?" Danielle walked Lancelot over for a closer look at the damage.

"That's exactly what I think." He crouched and ran his hand along the damaged post. "Someone rammed this with a piece of big equipment." He took out his cell phone and started punching.

"Are you calling Langley?"

"There's a hole here big enough to move troops through, and this fence didn't fall of its own accord. Langley's gonna want to know this like yesterday and he ain't gonna like it."

She waited while Riff got Langley on the phone and then had a choppy conversation.

"He was plenty upset," Riff said when he'd broken the connection. "He thinks Wade Hernandez may have run that big cattle hauler of his right through the fence and took what he wanted. I'll tell you right now, I would not want to be stamping around in Mr. Hernandez's boots."

"Langley can't be certain Wade is responsible for breaking down the fence."

"No, but he's got a feeling about this one. I expect he's right."

"How will he prove it?"

"I don't know, but he will. Him or Branson. You don't go stealing the Randolphs' cattle."

"They're not *Randolph* cattle," she corrected him. "They belong to whoever inherits this ranch. That could be me."

"All the same, Langley's running this ranch now. He's as nice a man as he can be as long as you don't mess with what's his. If you cross that line, then he's just like all the other Randolphs. You better step out of his way."

The description bothered her. It was too much like what Samuel had said about Langley, that he'd made himself Danielle's caretaker when he had no business doing so. And Samuel was partially right. Langley had told her where to live, where she could go. He'd even provided one of his men to follow every move she made. And he'd taken over the operations of her ranch.

She pushed the troubling thoughts aside. Langley was the good guy. She wouldn't let herself see him any other way. "What did Langley want you to do about the fence?"

"Wait on him. He said he's just down the road. He was already on his way to the Running Deer when he took my call."

So he had gotten her message and, just as she'd expected, he wasn't about to leave her to talk to Kincaid on her own. She wiped her sleeve across her forehead. The sun was beaming down on them. "It's warm for November," she said. "Is it always like this?"

"Not always, but lots of times it's just this hot when we're celebrating Christmas."

"Why don't we wait for Langley over by the Simpson place? We could stand in the shade of that persimmon tree."

He nodded and dropped the piece of barbed wire he was examining. "You go ahead. Just don't go off anywhere else. Langley would have my hide if he came back and found I'd let you get out of hollering range."

"And we don't want to upset him."

"Not if we can help it."

Danielle rode away, angry with herself for letting Riff plant seeds of doubt about Langley. He wasn't trying to take over; he was only trying to help. And she didn't just think that because she'd fallen in love with him. She thought it because it was true.

DANIELLE REINED IN Lancelot and slid from the saddle. "You get a break," she said, rubbing his neck and then looping the reins over a low-hanging branch of the persimmon tree. "You can wait in the shade."

Leaving the horse behind her, she walked around a huge pear cactus and stepped through what was once a door. Huge chunks of wall were missing from the structure as well as sections of the roof, so the place was dingy but not really dark.

Still, she cringed as something scurried in a back corner, then breathed easier when a squirrel dashed out and jumped through the missing window.

"Okay, Milton, if you were hiding a box in here, where would you put it?" Turning around slowly, she tried to picture her uncle doing the same, looking for the perfect hiding place. She felt a sudden chill wash over her like being in the shower when the hot water ran out.

A video. There was something about a video. Her head hurt, a nagging pain in her left temple that hadn't been there a minute ago. She leaned against the bricks of the fireplace, suddenly dizzy, nauseous.

Drawing in a deep breath, she willed her pulse to

slow. She had to think, had to pull some meaning from the words and phantom images darting crazily through her mind. Seconds later, she faded into another time and place. She was talking to Milton. He had something for her. A box. Insurance. A video of a murder.

The memories bucked wildly inside her mind and then disappeared like cunning ghosts. She closed her eyes and tried to retrieve them, tried to remember exactly what Milton had said to her.

But the images had vanished, back into the dark caverns where she couldn't follow. She forced her legs to move, to carry her to the back room of the house. She might as well look around while she was there. A pile of blankets lay in the corner, a fast-food bag sitting on top of them.

Footsteps sounded behind her. She turned, and her heart jumped into her throat. She was no longer alone.

Chapter Eleven

"Good afternoon, Danielle. Fancy running into you out here. And without your friendly bodyguard at your heels."

"Corky." She started to call for Riff but hesitated. He wouldn't be able to see them inside the house as he approached. If Corky was the one behind the trouble, she might be leading Riff into a trap.

She backed toward the door she'd come in. If she handled this right, she could lure Corky outdoors to the side of the house where Lancelot was tethered. That way, Riff would see them as soon as she called to him and not be blindsided.

"It was such a nice day that I hated to stay inside the cabin," she said, keeping her voice steady and reasonably friendly.

Corky propped his hand against a leaning wall. "But at least you have a cabin. The advantage of being a beautiful woman who fires Langley Randolph's engine. Me, I live in the decaying ruins."

"You're actually staying here?" She glanced around the dilapidated structure and then peered at the sunlight that streamed through gaping holes in the roof. "This place is falling down."

"I didn't say I lived well. I'm making it, though, and I don't hold my plight against you. This whole idea of leaving both of us the ranch sounds like something Milton would cook up. It's probably his idea of family humor."

She stepped over a loose board, moving closer to the opening where the door used to be. "Why are you staying out here? You said you were afraid to be on the ranch with a lunatic on the loose."

"I don't have a lot of choice. I'm a little short of cash at the moment." He spread his palms. "You know, sweetie, busted. Besides, I have an equalizer." Bending, he reached into his right boot and pulled out a small pistol. After toying with it, he pointed it at her and then toward the pile of blankets in the corner.

Fear churned inside her. She struggled not to let it cripple her ability to reason. "Where's your car?" she asked, striving for nonchalance. She failed miserably. Her voice cracked on the words.

"Parked behind that thick cluster of mesquite behind the house." He glanced over his shoulder. "I'm surprised no one's discovered it before now and tried to kick me off the property. You know, for a small ranch, there are a lot of cowboys nosing around."

"There shouldn't be, not anymore. Langley took over the management of the ranch."

He grinned. "Such a great guy, isn't he? What's in it for him, besides you, of course?"

"You're way off base. Langley is just being a good neighbor and looking out for me."

"Yeah, right, and you sound like a woman who might be interested in buying some oceanfront property in Tulsa."

"I have no reason not to trust Langley Randolph."

"You don't have any reason not to trust me, either, but you obviously don't." Corky took a step toward her. "You should, you know. I'm just like you, sweetheart. I want whatever I can get out of Milton Maccabbe's death. I sure didn't get anything out of him while he was alive except a hard time. Neither did my mom."

"Is that why you faked the will?"

Corky's laughter echoed around her. They could have been two friends sharing a joke. Only the tie that bound them wasn't friendship but an uncle she couldn't remember. An uncle who'd somehow led her into a frightening web of danger.

"You're a fine one to be hurling accusations at me," Corky continued. "Milton never had a niece or any other family. And even if he had, they'd have disowned him years ago."

"You don't know Milton that well. Your mother wasn't married to him for very long."

"I know *about* him. That's enough for me." Corky walked over and perched on the sagging window frame.

Danielle stepped back, moving into the rectangle of sunlight that crept through the opening. "What is it that you think Milton did that would make my family disown him?"

"I don't know about your family, sweetheart, but mine doesn't take too well to murder even though Milton did make it a profitable operation. When he was married to my mom, it paid really well. Not that he shared it, mind you. When we left, we ran with nothing but the clothes on our backs."

"And so you're bitter. You'd like to get back at Milton for the trouble he caused you and your mom. I can understand that."

"I passed the bitter stage years ago. I'm downright rotten now."

"So why are you here, Corky? Milton's dead. You can't get back at him."

"Like I told you, I'm here for the same reason you are." He twisted the bill of his faded baseball cap. "We could team up. It would make more sense than our fighting each other."

She backed closer to the opening. Thunder rumbled in the distance, yet the sun was still bright overhead. The contrast matched Danielle's mood. She wanted to close her mind to the picture of her uncle that Corky was painting, and yet she had a sinking feeling that what he was saying was laced with threads of truth. She stuffed her hands in her back pockets and met his gaze. "Do you think Milton has money hidden around the ranch?"

"No, he was too smart for that. He's likely got his fortune invested in a financial institution out of the country."

"Then what are you looking for?"

"I don't know. You tell me. From what I hear, someone is determined to run you off the ranch. So I figure there's something hidden here that's worth finding."

Her mind was swirling with doubts. Could she be wrong about Corky? Had he just pegged the situation the same way she had? There was something of value hidden on the ranch. A metal box. A video. The memories flooded her mind. She stumbled outside and into the sunshine and fresh air.

Corky followed her. "Hold on a minute, Danielle. I'm not through talking to you and I don't like being brushed off like some pesky spider."

Spider. The word conjured up a frightening image.

Apprehension sharpened her senses. "Don't try anything, Corky. Riff is over there by the downed fence. He has his back to us now, but all I have to do is yell and he'll be here in seconds."

"That old man. You surely don't think I'm afraid of him, though you probably should be."

"I'm not afraid of Riff and I'm not afraid of you." Only she was and she was sure he sensed it. She turned and walked toward Lancelot, away from the house so when she called to Riff, he would look up and see both her and Corky. Only Corky had a gun, and she wasn't sure the old cowboy was a match for him.

That second of hesitation was all Corky needed. He grabbed her with one hand and slammed the other over her mouth. She tried to scream, but her voice was strangled silent by the meaty flesh of his hand. He pushed up against her, and she could feel his acrid breath on her flesh.

Images came pounding into her mind. Huge fists smashing against her face and skull. An excruciating pain in her side. She was screaming, but no one heard her. And all she could see were two glazed eyes staring at her through a sea of black. Her legs gave way and she sank to the ground.

Corky yanked her back to her feet. "Don't go fainting on me."

She bit her bottom lip as reality took over again. This was no time to get lost in memories of the assault. Corky was much stronger than she was, but she had to fight. Her life was just beginning. Her life with Langley.

Danielle took a deep breath and called on every ounce of strength. She raised her knee hard and delivered a blow to his crotch. Corky stumbled back, yelping in pain. Danielle started to run for Lancelot, but one look at Corky and she knew she had to finish the job. Gritting her teeth with determination, she reached out and shoved Corky's writhing body. His feet slipped out from under him and he landed in the clutches of the prickly cactus.

His disgusting obscenities followed her as she dug her heels into Lancelot's sides and took him to a full gallop. The sorrel raced like the wind, as if he understood they were running from the devil himself. But Corky wouldn't be following, not with the sharp spines of the cactus firmly embedded in his back and behind.

She shuddered as Lancelot pounded toward Riff. One day, she might laugh at the memory of Corky squirming around in that cactus, looking like a porcupine. She might laugh at the expression on his face when he realized she'd one-upped him.

One day, but not yet. Still, it was damn good to be alive.

LANGLEY DROVE ACROSS the fenced pasture, the limbs of a mesquite brushing against the side of his truck. There was no road out here, but he didn't need one. The dry south Texas dirt was as hard as asphalt.

He'd just talked to Riff again. He'd reported that the tire tracks around the busted fence were fresh. Even more incriminating, they were the size that might have fitted on the cattle hauler Wade had driven to the Running Deer the other night.

The man galled him to no end. Taking advantage of a dead man was bad enough. Taking advantage of a woman who was already faced with overwhelming problems was about as cowardly and low as a man could go.

But unless he was badly mistaken, that was exactly what Wade Hernandez had done. Only he'd made a big mistake. A few phone calls to the auction houses and

Langley would be able to discover not only how many of Milton's steers had been sold but at what price. And that was how much money Wade would cough up to Danielle. She could use the cash herself. She could also press charges.

Riff met him at the truck before he'd even killed the engine. "I thought you'd want to see the fence for yourself. That's why I called you right away."

"You thought right. Fortunately, I was already on the property. I was coming out to meet with Kincaid and Danielle. Now she'll have something of interest to chat with him about."

Riff shook his head. "He's gonna be spouting steam. Kincaid may not be worth a plugged nickel, but he don't go stealing cattle from his own neighbors and he won't have his hired men doing it, either. You can bet Wade will be job huntin' come sunup."

"He better be hunting for a lawyer."

"You don't think Wade's the one who hung that dummy in the bunkhouse, do you? I mean, that's stretching it some. Whoever dressed that dummy in Danielle's clothes has to be the man who beat her up in New Orleans. Wade wouldn't have any cause to go that far just to make a few extra dollars."

"I don't know what to make of this, Riff. Believe me, I wish I did." Langley looked toward the fence. "Where's Danielle?"

"She rode over to the Simpson place to see if she could find a little shade."

Langley turned and saw Danielle and Lancelot racing toward them. He hated the fact that she had to face more trouble, but at least the timing was good, what with Kincaid on his way over. But one look at her face and he knew there was more wrong than just a few lost steers.

He grabbed Lancelot's reins in his right hand and Danielle's wrist with his left.

"Corky Westmorland is staying in the old Simpson place," she explained before he had a chance to ask.

Langley helped her from the saddle. "I told him to stay away from here."

"Well, he didn't. He's camping out inside the ruins of the house. We talked for a few minutes about my uncle. When I started to leave, he grabbed my arm and told me he wasn't through talking."

Acid pooled in Langley's stomach. He'd had about all he could stand without planting a fist against someone's jaw. He was sick of playing sheriff and of all the restraints that put on him. Not that he'd ever been a violent man, but then, he'd never had to go up against lunatics to protect a woman.

"Why didn't you holler?" Riff asked. "Like I told you to do. I could have been there before the man could sneeze twice."

"He had a gun. I didn't want to pull you into a trap. And once I was outside so you could see what was going on, he held his hand over my mouth. But I took care of him. I placed a knee appropriately and then shoved him into a giant pear cactus. I'm surprised you didn't hear him yelping."

Langley tried to concentrate on Danielle's words, but his impulse was just to go gunning for Corky like a lawman in an Old West shoot-out.

"I want you to go back to the cabin," he said, "and stay there until I get back."

"What are you going to do?"

"Arrest Corky and stick him in jail. It shouldn't be too difficult. He probably took off to hide in the brush, but a man with a rear end full of cactus spines isn't going to run too fast or too far, and he won't be sitting behind the steering wheel of a car.''

"He was a fine sight, decked out like a porcupine in his best quills.'' She smiled, but her shaky voice gave her away. She'd been frightened and rightly so.

Langley tugged his hat low on his forehead. "I need to take your horse, Riff. It'll be better for searching in the brush. You can take Danielle back to the cabin in my truck.''

"What about Lancelot?'' she protested.

"Don't worry about the horse,'' Riff said. "He'll make it home just fine on his own.''

"I don't expect Corky to get away from me, but if he does and shows up at the cabin…'' Langley threw up his hands. "If he shows up, do what you have to, Riff.''

"I read you loud and clear.''

Danielle stood beside Langley as he climbed into the saddle. "You can't go after him by yourself, Langley. Corky will be expecting you. He has a gun.''

"That makes two of us.''

"I'm going with you.''

"Not this time.''

"But this is all because of me.''

He met her worried gaze. "You can get that out of your head right now. This is not because of you. It's because your uncle dragged you into the middle of his war. And you are not responsible for fighting his battles or mine. And until someone else takes over, I'm still the man in charge.''

"Then will you at least be careful? I think Corky may be behind everything. He's so bitter toward Milton and admitted he was here looking for something.''

Langley bent his head and touched her lips with his. "I'll be careful and I'll be back in one piece.''

"I'm counting on that."

And so was he.

"CALL THE DEPUTY," Danielle told Riff, the second Langley rode away. "Langley needs backup."

"The boss man don't like my running his business. Besides, I expect Langley can take care of himself. If I didn't, I'd be right behind him."

Of course he would. His allegiance was to the Randolphs, not to her. Still, her nerves were rolling like the distant thunder. No matter what Langley said, if something happened to him, it would be her fault. She was the catalyst that had entangled him in this snarl of danger and violence.

By the time they reached the cabin, she was jumpier than ever. Fortunately, Ryder was nearby, out at the corral feeding the horses. She breathed a sigh of relief. She wouldn't have to persuade Ryder to go after Langley. He'd fly to his brother's aid. And if one Randolph was a fierce opponent, imagine the odds against Corky with a Randolph posse of two on his tail.

JOSHUA KINCAID WAS standing in the doorway when Danielle finally climbed the steps to the cabin. He was not what she expected. His hair was a silvery gray, but it was power, not age, she saw reflected in the depths of his eyes and in the swagger of his stance.

"You look flushed," he said, reaching for her hand. "Is something wrong?"

"Everything."

"You poor dear girl. You've had nothing but trouble since you arrived in Kelman. Just tell me how I can help."

He led her to the sofa. His touch was gentle, almost

fatherly, and the words of explanation and frustration tumbled from her mouth in a babbling fashion that lacked coherency even to her ears.

He patted her hand. ''I'm sure Milton never meant for you to be faced with any of this. He's probably thrashing in his grave as we speak.''

''Tell me the truth, Mr. Kincaid. Was my uncle a killer?''

''A killer? Where did you get an idea like that?''

''Corky Westmorland said that he was, back when he was married to Corky's mother.''

Kincaid sat down beside her. ''Milton never talked about it, but I always suspected that he was not proud of his past. Still, I never took Milton to be a violent man.''

''But you don't know for a fact that he never killed a man?''

''No. I only know that the Milton Maccabbe who worked for me was loyal, dependable and a hard worker. That's all I ask of my employees. I never let a man's past dictate my actions. It's his present that I deal with. Milton gave me ten good years of service, taking over full responsibility for the operations of my ranch and leaving me to concentrate on my nightclubs. That's why I rewarded him with this ranch. It was the one thing he wanted at retirement, and I felt he had more than earned it.''

''But in all those ten years, he never mentioned me?''

''When he went to work for me, he told me there were no family ties or responsibilities that would interfere with his doing whatever the job required of him. I took that to mean he had no family. You were quite a surprise to me.''

''I seem to have been a surprise to everyone.''

"Let me get you a drink," he said, standing but still holding her hand in his. "I think you could use it. Is there some brandy in the house?"

"No, but there's a bottle of sherry in the kitchen cabinet. Mary Randolph brought it over yesterday with a care package of vegetables and beef from her freezer."

"Mary Randolph is a wonderful lady. If I'd met someone like her, or been lucky enough to have been the man to win her heart, I might be living happily on my ranch instead of involved with all the headaches of running seven Kincaid's nightclubs."

Danielle's mind was still out on the ranch with Langley and Ryder, but she didn't miss the wistfulness in Kincaid's voice when he mentioned Mary Randolph. She wondered if Langley knew that the man he mistrusted so vehemently held his mother in such high esteem.

"You sit here and relax," Kincaid said, giving her hand a final pat before laying it back in her lap. "I'll get the sherry."

"I should be doing that for you. You're the guest."

"Nonsense. After the problems you've already had, you need a little pampering."

Danielle watched as Joshua Kincaid disappeared through the kitchen door. Riff was in there, making himself scarce but not so scarce he couldn't respond in an instant to any sign of trouble. After this morning's encounter with Corky, she'd be lucky if he didn't follow her into the bathroom.

She heard the two men talking in low voices, but she paid no attention to what they were saying. She could only think about Langley and Ryder and their search for Corky. She should have gone with Langley no matter what he said. Anything was better than just sitting and waiting.

She stopped wringing her hands when Kincaid came back into the room and handed her the glass of sherry. She took a slow sip. The sweet aftertaste lingered on her tongue. Somehow its warmth evoked memories of the passion she'd shared with Langley last night. She barely knew him, and yet he was all she knew.

Was it the amnesia and the danger that had caused her to bind with him so quickly? Or would she have fallen under his spell no matter what had brought them together? Probably the latter. She couldn't imagine not falling head over heels for him.

But at another time in her life, she might have had something better to offer him than a woman in peril.

"So, what do you say?"

Danielle jerked to attention. Kincaid was obviously waiting for her to give him an answer, but she had slipped into her own thoughts so completely she had no idea what he'd asked.

"If you take my offer, you can leave all of this behind you now," he added. "You can walk away from Kelman and go back to Samuel Drummer or not, as you see fit."

"I'm sorry, Mr. Kincaid. Could you repeat that offer? My mind must have wandered."

"Of course. I said that I'm willing to give you a small down payment on the ranch. If and when the ranch is officially turned over to you, I'll give you the rest of a fair purchase price. If the ranch is determined to belong to someone else, then the money I've already given you will still be yours to keep. You can't lose."

"But you could."

"I'm willing to take that risk."

"Why?"

"Let's just say it's one last favor I can do for Milton. I believe he'd want me to help you escape the danger that seems to be attached to the Running Deer. This way, you can go on with your life."

Go on with her life, money in hand. All she had to do was sell the ranch to Joshua Kincaid. Put all this behind her, and go back to her life. Only she didn't have a life to go back to. This was the only life she knew.

"I'll think about your offer, Mr. Kincaid."

"Good, but don't think too long. My spells of generosity are sometimes short-lived. And I'd appreciate it if you could keep this offer under your hat. I don't like it to get out what an old softy I really am." He winked.

Kincaid stayed a while longer, making small talk about Kelman and about his life as a businessman. He was a charming and captivating man with fascinating stories to tell. Another time she might have appreciated his company, but today anxiety filled her mind and choked the life from her heart.

Langley was out there chasing a madman. And she wouldn't breathe easy until he walked through that door and until Corky Westmorland was behind bars.

She had no solid proof that Corky was the man who'd vandalized the house, who'd hung her in effigy, who'd planted tarantulas in her lemonade pitcher. She had no proof he was the man who'd attacked her and left her for dead in New Orleans, and yet every instinct she possessed insisted that he was. She'd felt it in the fear that engulfed her when he'd pinned her arms behind her back and in the way his foul breath had burned into her own lungs.

After Joshua Kincaid left, she joined Riff in the kitchen. They talked about the weather, the Harvest Night celebration, everything except what was really on their minds. And they both turned their heads frequently to stare at the clock on the kitchen wall and the hands that seemed to be moving in slow motion.

At the first sound of a truck engine, they both raced to the door. Langley pushed open the driver's-side door of his truck and stepped out. Alone. His drawn face had paled to a ghostly white. Blood covered the front of his shirt.

Riff stepped in front of her. "What happened?"

"We caught Corky, found him in a deep cluster of thorny brush still sporting his quills. He's in the truck." Langley's voice was hard, cold.

Danielle's stomach turned over. She could see Corky's blanket-wrapped body slumped over in the passenger side of the truck. "He looks hurt," she said. "He looks—"

"Dead." Langley finished her sentence and then walked past her, holding his bloodstained hands in front of him as if he couldn't bear to have them attached to his body.

She followed at his heels. "Then he did pull his gun on you?"

"No."

"You must have thought he did," Riff said, following Langley into the bathroom. "Neither you nor Ryder would ever kill an unarmed man."

"We didn't. Someone else did."

Danielle slumped against the wall. "But I just left him, and he was alive."

Riff looked at her as if she were some traitor who'd just slipped through the battle lines. "If Langley said he and Ryder didn't do the shooting, then they didn't do it."

"He wasn't shot," Langley said, "and he wasn't dead

when we found him.'' He tore the bloody shirt from his body and slung it across the tub. "He was still breathing. We tried to resuscitate him, but it was no use.''

Danielle's stomach pitched violently. "It was the cactus, wasn't it? *I* killed him.''

Langley's hands were slick with soap, but he reached out to her with his eyes. "It wasn't the cactus, Danielle. It was a knife, plunged into Corky's chest. Just like the one we pulled from the dummy.''

She closed her eyes to hold back the tears that burned at the back of her eyelids. If she let them start, they would never stop falling. The nightmare was hers, but it reached out to everyone who came near her. It had killed Corky Westmorland, and if it didn't end soon, it would destroy Langley the same way it was destroying her. There was only one way to stop it.

Let the madman win.

Chapter Twelve

It was late afternoon before Danielle had a few minutes alone with Langley. By that time, he and Gordon had spent additional hours at the crime scene, searching for any scrap of a clue. Corky had been officially declared dead and the body had been delivered to the morgue. Now they sat side by side in the porch swing at the Running Deer.

Langley nursed a mug of strong black coffee. "Branson will be home by this time tomorrow. None too soon to suit me, though I hate that he has to return from his honeymoon to deal with a murder case. I had hoped things wouldn't come to that."

"No. I thought it was *me* the lunatic was after. Only it's really the metal box he wants. I was just the person standing in his way of finding it."

Langley held his hand over the cup, trapping the steam. "He must have realized that Corky was looking for the box, too."

"Only Corky didn't even know there was a metal box," Danielle said, still trying to come to grips with the fact that he was actually dead. "He only suspected there was something hidden on the ranch that was of value, at least valuable to the killer."

"Did Corky tell you all of that today?"

"Among other things." Other ugly things that had helped her make up her mind about what she had to do now. "And I remembered some more bits and pieces concerning my phone conversation with Milton this afternoon. I'm sure the box has something to do with a video and insurance. And with a murder."

"A video." Langley leaned forward, propping his elbows on his knees. He lost himself in thought for long minutes before continuing. "Milton could have been using a video to blackmail someone."

"But why would the person he was blackmailing have attacked me in New Orleans, unless..." Danielle jumped up from the swing and turned to face Langley. "Unless he thought Milton had mailed me the video. He could have stolen my luggage and my purse, thinking he was getting the video in the process."

"And then, just in case you had already seen the video, he planned to kill you to keep you from talking." Langley knotted his hand into a fist. "It makes sense, sick, but believable."

Danielle wrapped her arms around her chest. "Then after the attack, he must have come back to the ranch to search for the missing evidence while I was in the hospital."

"I think you may have hit on something." Langley tugged her back down beside him. "You have to stop searching for the box. This is a police matter now."

"I agree."

Relief lightened the lines in his face. "Good. I'm glad you're ready to listen to reason."

"I'm giving up my search. I'm leaving Kelman."

"You're what?"

"I'm leaving Kelman."

"To go where? Surely you're not thinking of going back to Samuel Drummer at this point."

Go back to Samuel? The thought had never crossed her mind. She was shocked that Langley could think that now, after they'd made love. He had to know how she felt about him, but, under the circumstances, maybe it was best if he didn't. It would only make leaving that much harder.

"I talked to Joshua Kincaid today. He made me an interesting proposition."

Langley raked his fingers through his hair, his frustration obvious. "I forgot all about his wanting to talk to you. What kind of one-sided proposition did he make you? To pay for *half* the cattle his foreman stole?"

"We didn't discuss Wade. We talked about Mr. Kincaid's buying the Running Deer."

Langley stared at her as if she'd slapped him across the face. "You're talking about leaving for good, aren't you?"

"I don't know about for good. But it's time that I leave."

"You're right. There's really no reason why you'd want to stay in Kelman." He sipped his coffee and stared past her into the endless, flat grassland beyond the cabin.

She'd hurt him. She could see the signs of it etched in the new furrows in his brow and the tight lines of his mouth. But if she didn't leave now, she might destroy him completely. It might be *his* body that was carried to the morgue next. They were no closer to finding the man responsible for the murderous violence than they'd ever been.

And, as long as she was in danger, Langley would never back away from the situation. She knew him well enough to be certain of that. It was better to hurt his pride and wound his heart than to see him dead. "I'm not a rancher, Langley."

"I know. I never expected you'd stay forever. You're not the type of woman who could be happy stuck on a dusty south Texas ranch day in and day out." He ran his palm along the rough denim of his jeans. "Tell me about the offer."

She filled in the details as an invisible wall rose between them. He waited until she was finished before he commented.

"It sounds like a decent proposition, especially if Kincaid doesn't expect you to pay back the good-faith money if we find the ranch is not actually yours to sell. And as long as the fair price he offers is actually fair. You can run it by me first if you're interested in my opinion."

"Of course I'm interested in your opinion. Actually, I wanted to make sure you didn't want the ranch before I agreed to sell it to him. If you do, it's yours. That is, if it's mine to dispose of. All I'd need is a little stipend to get me started somewhere far away from here."

"Somewhere far away from here." He repeated her words as if he had to hear them twice to believe them. He shook his head. "We don't need the land. Kincaid doesn't, either, for that matter. He doesn't run cattle on half the land he owns now, but this was his land before he gave it to Milton. If he wants it back and you want to sell it to him, go ahead. It's probably the best thing for you."

It was the worst thing for her. She was amazed he couldn't see that, that he didn't realize that in losing him, she was losing everything.

"When will you be leaving?"

"I'm not sure. As soon as Mr. Kincaid and I can come to an agreement and sign the paperwork."

"Not until after Harvest Night, I hope. Mom would never forgive you. She's looked forward to your meeting the rest of the family."

"The celebration is only two days away. I'm sure the deal won't move that fast."

"Don't count on it. When Joshua Kincaid cracks a whip, a lot of men jump."

But not Langley. Danielle was sure he didn't jump to anyone's whip but his own.

He stood. "Why don't you get your things? I'll give you a ride to the Burning Pear. You might want to go to bed early tonight. A couple of FBI agents are in town. They want to meet with the two of us first thing in the morning."

"Why would the FBI want to meet with me?"

"All they told me is that it's about your uncle. Apparently, they've been watching him for a long time."

DANIELLE STARED AT the two men across the narrow space of the sheriff's office. She wasn't sure what she'd expected FBI agents to be like, but it wasn't this. Not only were they not intimidating, but they could have been anybody off the street. If that was the desired effect, it worked.

The man who'd introduced himself as Blake was tall, attractive, on the slim side. She guessed him to be in his mid-forties, about ten years older than the one called Roland.

Blake appeared to be the one in charge. He leaned back in his chair and crossed one leg over his knee. "What exactly do you know about the man you call Milton Maccabbe, Miss Thibodeaux?"

"Basically nothing more than the little I've learned since I arrived in Kelman. He was a loner, unsociable, though he was apparently an excellent foreman during the time he oversaw the operations of Joshua Kincaid's ranch. I have the letter he sent me, the one you just read. If I knew any more than that, the facts were lost to me when the amnesia swallowed my past."

Langley put down the pencil he'd been balancing between his fingers. "You said the man she calls Milton Maccabbe. Does that mean he was really someone else? Like George Lackland?"

"Exactly. How did you get that piece of information?"

"We found a birth certificate for George Lackland in Milton's safety-deposit box. We noticed the age was right and wondered if the name change was a possibility."

"It was. George Lackland was reportedly killed in South America thirty-five years ago, but in actuality, he reentered the country as Milton Maccabbe."

Danielle rubbed two fingers against her temple, trying desperately to make sense of what the agent was saying. "I checked George Lackland's family background myself," she said. "His mother was Mildred Lackland. She only had one child."

"His dad married again when George was eight years old," Roland explained. "That marriage resulted in the birth of one child, a girl named Colette Lee Lackland."

"And that's the Colette Milton spoke of in his letter, my mother?"

"So it appears right now." Blake leaned in closer. "Colette's mother, your grandmother, was married to Milton's dad up until he died. George was only seventeen at the time. He left home shortly after his dad's death and, as far as we can ascertain, never made contact with the family again.''

''That would fit what he says in the letter. But what about Colette? Where is my mother now?''

''For some reason, no information was ever collected on her. She was only nine when George's dad died. She wasn't part of the investigation. That's why we have nothing on you.''

''Then you don't know what happened to my mother after she grew up?''

''No, but I can check on that for you. I should be able to get back to you in a couple of days.''

''I'd appreciate that.''

Langley perched on the edge of his desk. ''So what happened after George left home?''

''I don't know what happened during his early years. It was about the time he changed his name to Milton Maccabbe that he came to the attention of the FBI. Our methods weren't as sophisticated back then, but the agency received information that suggested George was working as a professional hit man. Not for the routine Mafia hits. They did their own dirty work. Your uncle was suspected of doing really important jobs for big-name clients.''

Danielle felt sick, but this was no time to lose control. She hadn't wanted to believe Corky, but now she had to face the truth. ''What do you mean by big-name clients?''

''Dictators from foreign countries reportedly hired him to take out government leaders in this country, the ones who made life hard for them.''

''You keep using terms like 'suspected' and 'reportedly.' Does that mean you have no proof that my uncle was guilty of these crimes?''

"That's exactly what it means. We've been watching George slash Milton for years. We've suspected him as the hit man in many situations but were never able to get the evidence we needed."

"Doesn't that suggest to you that your accusations may be faulty? He could be innocent," she insisted.

Blake shook his head. "It suggests to us that he was very, very good at what he did. You see, he had a unique way of keeping people quiet who might be tempted to testify against him. From what we've been able to surmise, he always gathers information to hold over their heads, seriously damaging information that would put them away right along with him. In addition, they are just plain afraid of a man who kills and never gets caught."

"Did someone tell you that?"

"More than one. For example, we tried to get Corky Westmorland's mother to testify against him years ago. She said she was not ready to commit suicide. We offered protection, but she insisted our protection was a joke against a man like Milton."

Evidence. A video. A murder. The memories made sense now. Perfect, nauseating, terrifying sense. She had no choice but to cooperate with the FBI. She spent the next half hour explaining what she had remembered about the metal box that her uncle wanted her to recover. Explaining her attack, the vandalism, the dummy, the spiders. And now Corky's death.

"How did you happen to reopen the case against Milton now?" she asked when they'd finished questioning her about every aspect of the past few weeks.

"You can thank Langley Randolph for that," Blake said. "As far as we knew, Milton had given up his illustrious career as a hit man when he came to work for

Joshua Kincaid. We backed off, but when the sheriff's office down here started investigating Milton Maccabbe, red flags went up all over the department.''

"You said it," Roland agreed. "For a part-time lawman, Langley is one thorough investigator."

"Not part-time," Langley corrected. "Temporary, and almost retired. Almost, but not quite."

"Well, in case you miss the work, come see us when this is over," Blake said. "We can find a spot for you."

"No thanks. I'm just a plain old cowboy and I like it that way."

"We'd refer to you as a powerful rancher," Roland said. "Just to keep the record straight."

Cowboy? Rancher? That wasn't the issue here. Danielle massaged her right temple. "The madness and danger aren't over yet. Nothing will be over until the man who killed Corky and tried to kill me is arrested."

"Right," Blake agreed. "We have to apprehend the murderer and locate the metal box he's willing to kill for. But your part is done. Yours and Langley's. All you have to do now is back off and let us handle it from here on out."

"That sounds great," Langley said, "but just how do you plan to handle it?"

"We're checking out a lot of things and several different people. Samuel Drummer for one. We want to know if he could have been in New Orleans at the time of the attack on Danielle."

"We checked the airlines," Langley said. "There was no record of his taking a commercial flight. And he has a firm alibi for the night of the attack, so he couldn't have driven back."

"Like I said, you're a thorough investigator for a novice, Langley, but we have a few more resources at our disposal.''

Langley leaned forward. ''In the meantime, it isn't safe for Danielle to stay on her own ranch.''

''We're aware of that,'' Blake said. ''And, like I said, we're working on it.''

Langley walked to the front of his desk. ''You've been doing that for thirty-five years.''

''What are you trying to say, Langley?''

''I'm saying that you just keep doing your job and I'll keep doing mine. I don't have thirty-five years of patience in me.''

The facts roared through Danielle's mind. Her past was marred by the brutal scars of violence. Once again, she doubted if she ever wanted to know the truth about herself. The only thing she was sure of was that she had made the right decision. No matter how she felt about Langley, no matter how he felt about her, she couldn't bring the kind of baggage she carried into his life.

She would turn the ranch over to Joshua Kincaid as soon as possible. She had no idea where she'd go, but it would be a long, long way from Kelman, Texas. She no longer felt driven to find the metal box her uncle had wanted her to have. If the FBI was right about him, he was a killer and his secrets were dirty and perverse.

The only thing left for her to do was to call Joshua Kincaid. And to go somewhere and sit quietly while her heart finished breaking.

THE HARVEST NIGHT celebration was well under way by the time Langley and Danielle reached the rodeo grounds. Toe-tapping fiddling music blended with laughter and a cacophony of voices. Bright-colored paper streamers danced in the light breeze and folding tables and chairs dotted the grassy area behind the rodeo viewing stands.

It was a night of celebration, and she was determined to keep it light. In all likelihood, it would be the last night she would ever spend with Langley and his family, and she wouldn't ruin it with sadness and recriminations. She had even worn her red dress and she planned to dance the night away in Langley's arms. There would be plenty of time for tears later when she was all alone. When she faced the fact that the only past she knew about was the one that tied her by blood to a paid assassin.

She ducked as a Frisbee sailed by her head.

"Sorry, miss. It got away from me." A preteen grinned at her sheepishly. "'Cause my brother can't throw it right."

"No problem." She picked it up and sailed it back to the brother.

"Nice arm." Buck Bogards stepped alongside them. "And the rest of you looks mighty fine, as well."

"Why, thank you. You look pretty cool yourself."

He beamed. "My wife picked out this shirt. She was tired of my work denims." He turned to Langley and clapped him on the shoulder. "Good to see you, too. Guess you're glad to turn the criminal-catching duties back over to Branson now that he's home."

"I never thought cows would look so good."

"Well, stop by our table later and get a piece of Martha's peanut butter fudge. Bring Danielle with you. Martha's dying to meet her."

Langley promised to see Buck later, the same way he did the next half-dozen or so men who stopped him on their way to the family picnic spot. Finally, she spotted the Randolphs, the whole clan stretched out on Mexican blankets and folding chairs. And right in the middle of them was a long folding table piled high with food.

Danielle tugged Langley to a stop. "Tell me who's who," she said.

"The tall lady in the blue skirt and white peasant blouse is Dillon's wife, Ashley."

"Actually, I met her today. She stopped by the house while I was helping your mother cook."

"What did you think of her?"

"She's every bit as nice as you said she was. I can see why your mother loves her like a daughter."

"Mom would love the Wicked Witch of the West if she gave her grandchildren, but Ashley is a super lady. I knew you'd like her. You'll like the rest of the family, too."

"I'm sure I will." The fact that they would even speak to her after the trouble she'd caused was reason enough to love them. She pointed toward a man standing in front of Mary's chair. "Who's the tall guy in the pale yellow shirt?"

"That's Dillon, the one who's married to Ashley. He's giving a short speech later tonight. At least he's promised it will be short. You can never trust a politician when it comes to the length of their speeches."

"He's very handsome, but he doesn't look old enough to be a senator."

"A senator and a dad. Petey is the spitting image of him."

"Where is his son?"

"Around here somewhere. Dillon had him with him in town today. Petey was already so excited he could barely sit still a minute."

"Then the other couple must be Branson and Lacy."

"Right. They're the newlyweds."

Mary spotted them and waved them over. Ready or not, Danielle was about to meet the rest of the Randolph clan. She knew they would be nice to her for Langley's sake, but underneath the facade of acceptance, they would be thankful she was leaving town soon. How could they not be?

She took a deep breath and held on to Langley's hand as he led her into the circle of his family.

"MAY I HAVE ANOTHER chicken leg, Grandma?" Petey galloped up to the table for the umpteenth time, his dark hair rumpled, his shirt pulled loose from his jeans.

"You certainly can," Mary answered him. "Do you want some potato salad to go with it?"

"No, ma'am. I don't have time. We're playing chase and I have to get back so Sarah can catch me. But I'll be back when you cut the chocolate cake."

"Sorry, pardner. You're too late. The cake's all gone," Langley teased.

"No, it's not. You wouldn't let them eat it all before I got mine. Right, Grandma?"

"No way," she assured him. "When Langley finishes cranking that ice cream, we'll haul out the desserts. I'll make sure you're here."

Ryder reached over to grab another piece of chicken while Mary had it uncovered. "So is that little redheaded girl you've been chasing your girlfriend?"

Petey giggled. "I don't have a girlfriend. I just like to let them catch me and then I run away again. But if you pull Sarah's braids, she'll sock you."

"I hope you didn't pull her braids," Ashley said, registering the appropriate amount of motherly shock.

"No, ma'am." He bit into his chicken leg and crumbles of breading showered down the front of his shirt.

He brushed them away with his free hand. "I don't want to get socked."

Ryder spooned up another helping of potato salad. "I see you're training that boy up right, Dillon. Let the girls catch you, but don't let them get their claws in too deep."

"I don't know. It looks like that sweet thing in your arms tonight has you wrapped around her little finger," Ashley teased.

"Guilty as charged," Ryder agreed. He shifted Betsy to the other knee, then grabbed his glass of tea a second before Betsy beat him to it.

Danielle relaxed. The Randolphs en masse were every bit as warm and friendly as they were individually. She knew Branson and Langley had spent the afternoon dealing with Corky's murder and other aspects of the investigation, but you'd never guess they had a thing on their minds tonight except enjoying themselves, their family and the hordes of neighbors who'd stopped by to chat. They were good performers.

The crowd quieted as the band returned to the makeshift stage after a lengthy break. The skinny, long-haired fiddle player ran his bow across the strings a few times as if to get everyone's attention. A balding cowboy in a pair of polished boots and a fringed leather vest sidled up to the microphone. He knocked on it a couple of times to assure himself that it was working before he spoke into it.

"Now that your bellies are full—and I know they are because I've seen the food piled on those plates—it's time to shake the lead out of those boots and behinds and hit the sawdust. And I don't mean just the young'uns. You older folks can get out here, too. Show them young whippersnappers how it's done."

The band broke into a lively Texas two-step and the sawdusted area in front of the bandstand filled with couples. Mary tapped her toes to the music. Dillon walked over to Langley. "Do you want me to crank awhile?"

"You're just trying to get out of dancing," Ashley complained good-naturedly.

"The ice cream's about finished," Langley said, "but you can take a turn or two if you want. That way, you can brag about helping when we dig in."

"*And* I can get out of dancing."

Ashley shook her head. "We've been married too long," she teased. She grabbed Ryder's arm. "Come on, brother-in-law. Twirl me around the floor before one of your many admirers enlists your services."

Ryder handed Betsy to his mother. "Okay, but dancing with married women is not good for my reputation."

"What reputation?" Langley joked. He looked over at Branson. "Are you two lovebirds going to dance or are you just going to sit there staring into each other's eyes?"

"We're waiting for a belly rubber," Branson said. "Besides, I'm still sore from trying to keep up with that wild, exotic hula dancer at the luau last night."

"That hula dancer was me," Lacy quipped. "And he wasn't even close to keeping up."

"That's because you're good." He turned to Langley. "That wife of mine has moves I didn't know existed. Not that I'm complaining, mind you."

Lacy's cheeks turned from tan to red in record time. Danielle couldn't help envying her happiness.

The first song ended and the second started, another perky number that let the practiced swingers get in a lot of twirls and fancy footwork. Ryder and Ashley definitely fitted into that number. A group of women formed a group at the back of the dance area and started line dancing, tapping their toes and swinging their hips in unison.

Langley took Danielle's hand. "Would you like to dance? I'm a little rusty, but I'll try not to stamp on your toes."

"I'd love to," she said, only fearing that once she was in his arms, she'd never want to leave them.

He led her to the dance area. A minute later, she knew he was not rusty. He moved with the music, a cowboy tune that suited him perfectly. He twirled her and swung her and held her close, all so expertly she never missed a beat.

"You dance the way you do everything else," she whispered. "Sexy and perfect."

"It's an old cowboy custom. We only do what we do well. Everything else we leave for city folks." He leaned in close. "Besides, it's easy to dance when you have a gorgeous, talented partner. Did I tell you how beautiful you look tonight?"

"Once, but don't let that stop you."

He swung her again, then brought her back into his arms as the number came to an end. Another number started, this one slower, the belly rubber Branson had talked about. The dance area became crowded. Langley held her all the closer.

She laid her head on his shoulder as his hand tightened around her waist. His body pressed against hers, and the need inside her was so real and so strong she thought it might steal her breath away. But somehow she kept moving. She would do what she had to do. But she would never forget Langley Randolph. And she would never stop loving him.

Langley tightened his hand around Danielle's waist,

pulling her closer. Everything was wrong and yet she felt so right in his arms. She didn't feel like a woman who was leaving. She felt like a woman who'd settled in to stay.

Only she would soon be gone. It wasn't his life she'd taken up permanent residence in, but his very soul. He felt a tap on his shoulder. He turned to find Samuel staring at him.

"Do you mind, Langley, if I have one dance with *my* fiancée before I concede defeat?"

He ached to refuse the man, but how could he? He finally knew how Samuel must feel. Losing Danielle was enough to tear the heart right out of a man. He placed Danielle's hand in Samuel's and slowly backed away.

"Quaint celebrations they have in these small towns," Samuel said, circling Danielle's waist with his hand. "Hopefully, they'll be enough for you. Rural festivals and Langley Randolph."

"I'm leaving Kelman, Samuel."

He lost the rhythm and missed a couple of steps. "When did you decide that?"

"In the past day or two. I'm turning the ranch back over to Joshua Kincaid."

His eyes narrowed. "Where will you go?"

"I haven't decided. Just away, that's all I know. I'm sorry if I hurt you, Samuel. I really am. But I'm not the woman you used to know. Even if my memory returns, I won't be."

The music stopped. Samuel put his hands on her shoulders and met her gaze. "I'll miss you, Danielle. But I'm glad you're leaving the ranch. There's something evil about that place. It's destroying you." He held on to her hand as they walked from the dance area. "If you change your mind about us," he said, "you know where to find me."

"I know, but I won't be back, Samuel."

"Then I guess this is goodbye." He touched his lips to her cheek and walked away without looking back. Funny, but she could have sworn the look she'd seen in his eyes was one of pure relief that everything between them was finally over.

"Miss Danielle, Uncle Ryder is looking for you." She turned to find Petey a step behind her.

"He is? What does he want?"

"He has a family annesment to make."

"You mean an announcement?"

"Yeah, one of those. He said he can't do it until you get over there to hear it. And Grandma says we can't eat the ice cream or have any cake until Uncle Ryder tells his news." Petey took her hand and pulled her along. "So we have to hurry."

"I guess we do. I wouldn't want to miss a family announcement."

"And *I* don't want the ice cream to melt."

The entire Randolph clan had gathered by the time Danielle and Petey reached the picnic spot. Branson, Langley and Dillon were talking, Lacy and Mary were packing away food and Ashley was changing Betsy's diaper.

Ryder was pacing. He stopped as they approached and walked over to stand beside his mom. "Okay, I need everybody's attention."

"You can't be getting married," Branson teased. "You didn't even bring a date."

"But he's got that look in his eye," Langley said. "Either he's pregnant or he won the lottery."

Ryder smiled and put up his hand. "All right, you

guys. Have your laughs. When you're through, I'll make your day.''

Danielle stood at the back of the group, acutely aware that she had no real right to be there for this. As if reading her thoughts, Langley stepped to her side and put a hand on the small of her back.

"I don't know how to say this," Ryder began. His voice seemed strained, his muscles tense.

This was a serious, almost somber, side of Ryder that she had never seen. Evidently, the rest of the family were just as surprised by the change in him. No one spoke. No one moved. Not even Petey. Ryder had no choice but to finish what he'd started.

"I know how you all feel about Betsy," he said, exhaling sharply in punctuation. "We all want her to know and to be with her real parents."

Danielle looked over at Mary Randolph. One hand was over her heart, the other over her mouth, as if to keep from crying out. In her mind, Betsy was her granddaughter. If Ryder was about to tell them differently, it would break her heart.

Ryder stood in front of them, his words suspended in air that was thick with tension. Rocking back on his heels, he sucked in a ragged breath before laying a hand on his mother's shoulder. "I hope you're all ready for this because the proof is finally in. I know who Betsy's parents are.''

Chapter Thirteen

Ryder exhaled sharply. A week ago, he'd never expected to be standing there with news like that. But Danielle's interest in his past had sent him dredging up old memories. And those old memories had been enough to set the wheels of possibility in motion.

It couldn't have happened, but yet it had. Betsy couldn't be his daughter. But...

He squeezed his mom's shoulder. "I'm Betsy's father."

A hush fell over the Randolphs, one so complete it was as if they'd been frozen by some psychic phenomena. Finally, Mary broke the silence, squealing and throwing her arms around her youngest son. Ryder held her close as tears streamed down her cheeks.

Then as if it had been choreographed for a grand finale, Ryder's three brothers and his sisters-in-law mobbed him, smothering him in hugs. Danielle found it hard to swallow. So much happiness, so much love.

A family. That said it all.

But she wasn't part of their family and she had no right to be there at a time like that. The Randolphs had solid roots, grounded in principles and love. She was the niece of a man who murdered innocent people for money. And that was all she knew of who she was.

She stayed in the background as Ryder's family pummeled him with questions. He kept his answers simple, basically telling them the same story he'd told her. He had been seeing a woman when he'd had the accident that ripped up his knee and put his rodeo career on hold. He'd thought he was in love with her and that she was in love with him, but he'd obviously misread the signs.

He'd never seen or heard from her after the accident, and he hadn't even considered the fact that she might have gotten pregnant until just recently. They'd used protection *almost* every time. But once the doubts surfaced, he hadn't hesitated to do what he had to in search of the truth.

"DNA testing doesn't lie," Dillon agreed, when Ryder explained the blood tests.

Langley threw an arm over Ryder's shoulder. "Looks like my little brother is a dad." His last four words were almost lost in the emotion that choked his voice.

"And Betsy really is my granddaughter," Mary said. She was holding the baby girl now, brushing the wispy brown curls away from her pudgy little cheeks. "I knew she was. I loved her from the very first moment I held her in my arms."

"Yeah, but I guess her mother didn't feel that way," Ryder said. The bitterness crept in, slight, but still enough to notice.

"Don't be so quick to judge, Ryder." Ashley took his hand. "You don't know her heart. Sometimes it takes more love to let go than it does to hold on."

Danielle watched the scene around her, but her heart folded itself around Ashley's words. Sometimes it did take more love to let go. And that was what she had to do. She carried a legacy of violence that ran too deep to escape and she would not pull Langley or his family into it.

She loved him enough to let go.

DANIELLE LAY AWAKE for hours, the big house at Burning Pear groaning and settling around her. Her body was tired, yet thoughts of the strange events of the past few weeks tumbled about in her mind and refused to be silenced.

If her fragmented memories were accurate, somewhere on the Running Deer was a box that might unlock the mystery of Milton Maccabbe. A box that someone wanted so desperately he'd tried to kill Danielle. When that hadn't worked, he'd tried to frighten her off the land. But who? And was it only the evidence he wanted, or was killing her part of some man's final payback to Milton Maccabbe.

She beat her fists into her pillow. The day after tomorrow she was to meet with Joshua Kincaid. She would sign a paper of intent to sell him the ranch if and when it became hers to sell. In exchange, he would give her five thousand dollars to help her start her new life.

The FBI planned to take over the investigation surrounding Corky's death and search for any incriminating evidence that might be hidden on the ranch. And once she was gone, Langley would let them. He and his family could return to the peaceful lives they'd enjoyed before she appeared on the scene.

She rolled onto her back and started counting sheep. But all she saw was Langley. He was walking toward her across a grassy pasture. She loved his swagger, the tilt of his Stetson, the way he filled out his jeans. His smile as he stepped close.

No matter what she might discover when the amnesia lifted, those were the images that would haunt her forever.

But Langley disappeared. Now there was a woman walking and stretching her neck to get a better look at the plants hanging from the balcony above her head. A few strands of purple and gold Mardi Gras beads were trapped in the iron railings and meandering vines. They dangled precariously as if tempting some passerby to try to leap up and retrieve them.

But it was growing dark, and she needed to get back to her hotel. She stopped to check her bearings underneath the glow of a streetlight and then hurried to take a shortcut back to the hotel. The streets were empty. They had lost their sense of magic.

Footsteps sounded behind her. She had to hurry. Run. Get away. Only her body wasn't moving. She was trapped. Trapped. Trapped.

Danielle jerked to a sitting position. Sweat pooled between her breasts and rolled from her brow. The nightmare had come calling again and this time a hundred times clearer than ever before.

She longed to tiptoe to Langley's room and knock on his door. Ached to crawl into his arms and feel the strong beating of his heart. Craved the passion they'd shared in this very bed. But she had no right to reach out to him until she was sure that doing so would not endanger his life. And not until she knew she had something of value to offer. And that day might never come.

She threw her legs over the side of the bed, then went to the window and stared out into the dark shadows. Morning couldn't come too soon.

LANGLEY SAT AT the small desk in the family study, going over notes he'd scribbled on a legal pad. There had to be something he'd overlooked, some seemingly insignificant clue that would help him solve the puzzle.

The missing link was still the madman who wanted something that had been hidden on the Running Deer. Something hidden in a metal box.

Danielle had been obsessed with finding that box herself up until two days ago. Then she'd suddenly changed her mind and decided to run. Only she was the bravest woman he'd ever met. Fear only made her fight harder. Frustration added fuel to her determination.

There was only one reason she was running now—to protect him. To make sure he backed out of the investigation. Branson had figured it out. But now that Langley understood her motive, he wasn't about to let her walk away until he knew she was completely safe. The only problem was finding a way to stop her.

He was just about to leave when the phone rang. He picked it up and answered. It was Branson's voice on the other end of the line.

"We may have finally got a break in Danielle's case."

"Good. I was beginning to think this guy was too smart for us."

"No, they always slip up eventually."

"Milton didn't."

"He probably did, but no one caught the mistake. Anyway, I tracked down the company that makes the knives our killer used on Corky and on the dummy Danielle found hanging in the bunkhouse. They're made by a small company in a town south of New Orleans. It's owned by a Cajun man who was extremely helpful. He said most of his knives are sold in the immediate area."

"Does he export any to Texas?"

"Not a one. Which means they were probably bought

in New Orleans before our perp attacked Danielle and stabbed her with one of them.''

Langley played with an idea about a minute before it crystalized in his mind. He copied down the name and address of the knife company, then thanked Branson for calling. His next call was to Southwest Airlines. With any luck, he'd be in New Orleans by midafternoon.

His temporary stint as lawman had officially ended, but he was in this up to his eyeballs and he couldn't just walk away. Not when it was Danielle's life that was at risk.

DANIELLE STEPPED THROUGH the door and onto the front porch of the cabin at Running Deer. Three weeks ago, she'd stood in this very spot and shuddered, reluctant to step inside. Now she dreaded leaving it behind. But she'd made her decision and she wasn't backing out.

She hadn't seen Langley at all yesterday. According to Mary, he'd been off taking care of some out-of-town business. Danielle suspected he was avoiding her now that she'd made up her mind to leave. If so, he'd apparently changed his mind. He'd just called to say he was on his way over and that he wanted to talk to her.

The sun was bright, too hot for the fall of the year. She shrugged out of her cardigan and tossed it on the porch swing. Riff was feeding the horses, close by as always, just in case she needed him. A pistol was belted at his waist. A constant reminder that there was still a killer on the loose.

She leaned against the porch railing, the one that was strong and sturdy since Riff had finished with it, and waited for Langley. A few minutes later, he'd parked his truck under the splotchy shade of a scrubby oak and was heading up the walk.

"Grab your hat," he said, tipping his.

"What for?"

"We're going on a picnic at Branson Creek. I have the sandwiches all packed."

The cheeriness of his mood made hers seem all the more dour. "Going on a picnic won't make me change my mind about leaving, Langley."

"I know. You have to go. Brave amnesia sufferer risks life to save helpless cowboy next door."

"That's absurd."

"Is it? It doesn't matter anyway. That's not what we're going on a picnic to discuss."

"Then what are we going to discuss?"

"How I found out who murdered Corky Westmorland."

She heard his words, but it took long moments for them to sink in. Even when they did, she couldn't quite believe them. "Did you say you know who murdered Corky?"

"That's exactly what I said. Now, get your hat. I'll tell you all about it at Branson Creek."

"I STILL DON'T UNDERSTAND." Danielle sat next to Langley on the lightweight blanket he'd brought with them, her feet tucked beneath her. "If all you know is that the knives were made in south Louisiana, how does that help you?"

"I flew to New Orleans yesterday. I spent the afternoon cruising French Quarter shops checking for which ones might sell that particular brand of hunting knife."

"And did you find some?"

"I found three. In every one of the shops, I showed the salespeople Samuel Drummer's picture. I didn't mention the knives. I only asked if they remembered waiting on that man in their shop.''

Danielle's blood ran cold. "Surely it wasn't Samuel."

Langley reached over and took her hands in his. "When I showed the owner of the third shop Samuel's picture, he recognized him at once. Samuel had impressed him. A nice easygoing fellow who was exceptionally generous. He told the man he was buying the knives as Christmas gifts for all his hunting buddies."

"How many did he buy?"

"A half dozen. All exactly alike."

"Samuel." She shook her head as ugly images spun in her mind. "If it hadn't been for you, I might have gone with him that day in the sheriff's office. He could have finished what he started in the French Quarter."

"I'm just glad he never got that chance."

She laid her hand on Langley's arm. "But if it was Samuel, why didn't he kill me the night we were alone in the cabin?"

"I thought about that, too. But by that time he'd already let us know he was around. If he'd killed you at that point, he would have been the prime suspect. He was too smart for that."

"Too smart and a good actor. He played the part of worried fiancé so well." Her insides tightened as she remembered the times he'd told her what they'd been like together. She'd felt so guilty, knowing she didn't feel anything for him. Now she knew she'd never been him with him before. And with that thought, a new set of problems came hurtling through her mind. "If Samuel was lying about everything, then I was never engaged to him."

"Exactly."

"So the fact still remains—I could be married to

someone else. I could be anybody. I could have done anything."

"We always knew that was a possibility, Danielle, but we don't know anything for certain. Don't be so quick to grab more problems."

"I don't have to. They'll grab me." Plagued by a new wave of anxiety, she ran her hands through her hair. "So what do we do now?"

"Relax. Your memory may come back sooner since the danger is over. And it is *over*." He took one of her hands in his. "I gave the information to the FBI. They put Samuel under twenty-four-hour surveillance. They want to watch him and see what else they can learn before they arrest him. They think he's tied in with your uncle, that he was one of Milton's crew, so to speak."

"My uncle, the professional killer." She was glad now that she'd never met him.

"There's more news," Langley said, "though it pales by comparison."

"I guess it would. Does it involve Samuel?"

"In a roundabout way. It involves one of his victims. The FBI searched Corky Westmorland's apartment. They found a letter from Milton telling Corky he was dying and apologizing for any grief he might have caused him. Apparently, your uncle was trying to ease his conscience before he died."

"So that's how Corky knew Milton was dying."

"And the reason he decided to fake a will."

Danielle ran her fingers along the edge of the blanket. "Poor Corky. He held on to his bitterness for so many years that it finally cost him his life."

Langley stretched and stood. "Bitterness can do that to a man. But that's enough talk of unpleasant things. I brought you out here to celebrate the good news." Langley walked back to his horse and loosened the saddlebag. "I hope your appetite is in rare form," he said, pulling out plastic containers of food. "Mom packed the lunch and she doesn't understand the word 'light' when it comes to eating."

"Actually, I'm starved."

LANGLEY LAY BACK on the blanket, his hands behind his head. He'd been doing okay until he ate his fill of his mom's chicken salad sandwiches and coconut pie. The two glasses of wine hadn't helped, either. Now he was seriously feeling the consequences of getting only a couple of hours' sleep last night. He'd been too keyed up to sleep in New Orleans and he'd caught the red-eye into San Antonio that morning.

He was also feeling the effects of being with Danielle. It was impossible to be near her like this and not want her. He wrapped his fingers around her arm and tugged her down beside him. Her hair fell down around his face, all silky and smelling like springtime. He traced her mouth with his fingertips. "Did I ever tell you that you're the most beautiful neighbor I've ever had?"

"Is that why you like me, Langley? Because of the way I look?"

"That's part of it." He rose up on his elbow and stared into her eyes. "You are gorgeous," he said, trying to answer her question as honestly as he could. "But I've met lots of beautiful women. I didn't chase after them the way I have after you."

"What is it you see in me, Langley? I'm not fishing for compliments." She trailed her fingers along the front of his shirt. "Or maybe I am. It's just that I have so little to offer that I can't understand why you go to so much trouble for me."

"You have everything any man could want."

"Amnesia. Would any man want that? I could have done anything in my past. I may have committed crimes. It's for sure that the only relative I know about is a merciless assassin."

He laced his fingers through her hair and then massaged the tight muscles of her neck. "I don't know the Danielle who existed before. I only know you, the way you are now."

"But my past is part of who I am, the same way your past is part of you. I see your mom and your brothers and I understand you better. I watch them interact and I understand how you came to be the man you are. You're honest and dependable, solid and timeless, like that ranch you love so much."

"You make me sound like a Boy Scout."

"No, like a cowboy. Rugged, rock hard, sexy. I'll always think of you like that." She traced the line of his chin with her fingertips and he ached to pull her to him and silence her talk. It made him uneasy, made him think she was saying goodbye. He'd always known it would happen one day. A woman like Danielle would never be content to spend her life on a ranch in south Texas. But he hated that the one day had come so soon.

"You asked me what I like about you, Danielle. I'll tell you, and you can be sure it doesn't have a damn thing to do with what you did or were in your past." He ran his hand down her arm and then back up again, aroused as always by the softness of her.

"I like the way you make me feel. You can make me laugh or make me want to beat my fists into the wall in frustration, but you always make me feel something. You walk into a room, and my insides sizzle with awareness. You lay your hand on my arm, and I feel it clear to my toes.''

His heart beat like crazy in his chest. He wasn't used to talking about emotions. Hell, until Danielle had entered his life, he barely even had emotions. He was the steady, dependable, *dull* brother. He pulled her close and went weak with wanting her.

She leaned over and caught his lips with hers. He reeled with the taste of her, with the thrill of her breath mingling with his.

''Make love with me, Langley. Here, on the blanket under the warm Texas sun. Pretend we're just two ordinary people in love.''

She didn't have to ask twice.

Chapter Fourteen

Langley rolled over and tangled his fingers in the buttons of Danielle's blouse while his mouth found hers again. He kissed her lips, her eyelids, the tip of her nose, his body overcome by a need more powerful than any he'd ever imagined.

When he finished undressing her, she returned the favor. Her fingers singed into his flesh as she unzipped his jeans and slid her fingers down the length of his abdomen. He groaned and moved to help her. He shoved the rough denim fabric down his hips and over his aroused body, finally kicking out of them.

The sun beat down on their naked bodies, but he knew it was not the sun that had set him on fire.

"You do know how to throw a picnic," she whispered, melding her body into his.

"I'll bring the lunch and wine anytime as long as you're the dessert."

She straddled him. He was losing himself again, rocketing somewhere in outer space where his body had no weight and his heart drummed to some exotic, animal beat.

She moaned softly and whispered his name. And then

he was past hearing, past understanding, past everything but the searing blast of passion. Past everything except the realization that he might never know this kind of happiness again.

DANIELLE LAY VERY STILL and listened to the slow, rhythmic sound of Langley's breathing. He had fallen asleep. She didn't mind. She could stay here forever, just watching his beautiful bronzed chest rise and fall. But the longer she stayed with him, the harder it would be to leave. If Samuel was the killer, and it appeared that he was, then she would no longer be putting Langley in danger if she stayed.

But she couldn't begin to make a life with him until she knew who she was, what she had been. It wasn't fair to either of them.

She eased from the circle of his arms, careful not to wake him. Bending, she picked up her jeans and wiggled into them. Her bra was missing, probably lying under Langley's sleeping body. But there was no one but Langley to notice if she didn't wear one, and he wouldn't object at all. She shook the wrinkles from the white Western shirt and poked her arms through the sleeves.

A roadrunner zipped by in front of her, and she stopped to watch his frantic movements. This time, she hadn't even jumped when he'd come scurrying through the grass. The abundance of wildlife had ceased to startle her and now totally amazed her. It was another thing she'd miss when she left this place.

Grabbing her boots and socks, she padded through the short grass to the creek's edge. A fish jumped, breaking the surface and the silence. She stared into the golden ripples. The sun's reflection on the water was glaring, mesmerizing and yet disturbing.

A creek and then past that the remains of a house that had burned down years ago.

Danielle trembled as she yanked on her socks and pulled on her black boots. A hammering pain beat into her temples and she had to struggle for a decent breath of air.

An old well. Twenty yards north of the chimney. A metal box. A video of men being murdered.

She raked her hand through her hair, her fingers digging into her scalp. She wanted to scream, to run. To go—

No. She forced herself to suck in a deep breath. It was the memories again. Taunting her.

She shook her head to clear it. An old well. Had it been her uncle or Langley who told her about old wells? They were usually covered, only sometimes they weren't. You could fall into one and drown in the murky water.

Turning, she stared over the tops of the mesquite until she located the chimney of the old Simpson place. It wasn't far, a few minutes by horseback.

She backed away from the creek. Other thoughts were pouring into her head now, fragments, jagged edges of a puzzle that didn't fit into a whole. A rambling white house. People at a party. It was spring, and she was dancing in a gauzy dress.

But then the music stopped. Something was dreadfully wrong.

No, she couldn't think of that now. What was it that Milton had said about the box? Her head was spinning, thoughts coming at her from every direction. She had to sort them out, grab and hold on to the ones that made sense. She fell against a tree.

Get the box. Get the video. It will be your insurance.

Danielle reeled from the images. Moving as if in a trance, she climbed on Lancelot and raced across the yellowed grass while frightening memories churned inside her mind.

She reached the chimney in minutes, then slid from the saddle and threw Lancelot's reins over the same tree where she'd left him the other day. Had she been this close to the box and never known it? Had her subconscious been pulling her to this spot all the time?

Voices screamed in her head as she paced off twenty yards past the chimney. The well was there, just as it had been in the images that flashed through her mind. Falling to her knees, she peered inside. The hole seemed to drop away forever, a black pit that smelled of decaying vegetation and murky water.

She ran her fingers along the side of the inner wall. Somewhere there should be a metal box, but she had no idea how big it would be or how well hidden. If it was in the depths of the well, she'd never be able to retrieve it by herself.

One metal box, but it was important enough to her uncle that he had wanted her to come here and find it. Only Milton was a paid assassin, a man not to be trusted. A man who might be dragging her into even more nightmares.

Her heart pounded against her chest as her fingers roamed the side of the well, her nails digging into the earth. She could hear the loosened dirt falling for what seemed like an eternity before it splashed into the water below. But she had to be careful. The circumference was just big enough that she could slip into the hole and plunge into the water herself, as helpless as the clods of dirt that fell from her fingers.

A lump of clay dropped into her hand, and the tip of her thumb hit against something cold and metallic. It was the box.

THE PIERCING RING of Langley's cell phone woke him. He grabbed for it and barked a hello, all the while looking around for Danielle. A minute ago, she'd been beside him.

"Langley, this is Branson. I just got a call from Blake, the FBI agent."

"Good news, I hope."

"Good and bad. They've confirmed that Samuel did take a flight to New Orleans and they've placed him there at the time of the attack on Danielle. He traveled under an alias and a fake ID."

"And the bad news?"

"Samuel slipped the tail they had on him. The agent thought he was in his apartment sleeping. When Samuel didn't come out this morning, he finally got suspicious. He went inside, but Samuel was gone. Blake says they expect to locate him soon, but thinks we should keep an eye out for him."

But Langley was already breaking into a cold sweat. Danielle had been lying in his arms a short while ago. Now she was gone and so was Lancelot.

"I have another problem, Branson. Danielle's somewhere on the ranch and I don't know where to start looking for her."

"I'd try the cabin first if I were you."

AIR RUSHED INTO Danielle's lungs. The box was right where Milton had told her it would be. She scratched and dug in the dirt until she could get a grip on the corner of the box. She yanked as hard as she could.

The box gave and she fell backward, her bottom landing on the hard ground, her boots kicking into the air. She stayed there, sitting on the grass, box in hand, while she dug into her pocket and retrieved the key that she'd carried with her since the night the nurse had handed it to her in the New Orleans hospital.

She hesitated, the box in her lap, then inserted the key into the lock. Finally, fingers shaking, she turned the key and lifted the lid. She wasn't sure what she expected, but the contents appeared to be no more than junk mail stuffed into a private safe half the size of a child's lunch box.

A folded business-size envelope had been placed on top. She lifted it out so she could see the other contents. The envelope was sealed shut, and her first name was written on it in blue ink. A black velvet pouch was scrunched in the corner, and a video lay flat in the bottom of the box.

Scooting away from the edge of the well, she turned the envelope over. The dirt from her fingers made brown smudges against the white as she broke the seal and pulled out two pieces of paper.

The first one was a handwritten will. She skimmed the page. There were a few legal terms thrown in, but mostly it was written in plain English. Being of sound mind, Milton Maccabbe had left the ranch and all his material possessions to one Danielle Gaubert.

Danielle Gaubert. That was her name. A new rush of memories flooded through her. She had been so happy, dancing in the grass on their front lawn. She had just received her master's degree in international business. Life was waiting for her. So was a night of celebrating.

Only they had to wait until her mother got home to start the festivities, and her mother was late.

Her mother, the beautiful Colette Gaubert. But her mother hadn't come home that day. The small car she'd been driving had collided with a truck on the interstate.

Sadness washed over Danielle in a suffocating wave. She'd missed her mother so much. That's why she'd taken the job on another continent, hoping to put the hurt behind. She'd made a new life.

And then she'd gotten the letter from Milton Maccabbe.

Trembling, she slipped the will back into the envelope and stared at the second sheet of white paper. It was a letter addressed to her. Like the will, it appeared to have been written with the same shaky hand that had penned the letter the forensics team had found in her jacket pocket.

Dear Danielle,

If you've found this letter, then I know you made it safely to the Running Deer and that you got here after my death. I hesitated to write these things before. I was afraid if I did that you would never come here, and it is important to me that you do.

I never saw your mother after I left home at seventeen. It was better that way. My father had died, and I did not become the type of person your mother would have wanted to claim as her half brother. I made many bad choices during my lifetime. Like the cancer that eventually destroyed my body, the choices destroyed my soul.

But the one good memory I carried with me through all my life was your mother crying the day I left and begging me to stay. Colette was the only person who had ever truly believed in me. I let her down.

The day I left, she gave me her most prized possession, a Mardi Gras charm on a silver chain. She wanted me to have it for luck. I still have the charm, though my luck has played out. I'm leaving it to you. You'll find it in the velvet pouch. May it bring you the luck your mother once wished for me.

My affairs are in order. The ranch is mine free and clear, and I want you to have it. It is all I have. You may do with it as you wish. The money I sold my soul to make is all gone, squandered away. I'm not proud of what I've done, but it's too late for regrets.

Finally, I am leaving you a video that I hope you never have to watch. If it gets out, it would ruin the lives of some guilty and some innocent men, and I've done enough of that already. But the video will be your insurance. It is evidence of murders that have been committed by men who worked for me in the past. Some of them are vicious and vengeful, the kind who might try to hurt you once they realize you are kin to me. If anyone threatens you in any way, give this video to Sheriff Branson Randolph. He's an honest lawman. He'll know what to do.

> May God go with you.
> Your uncle,
> Milton K. Maccabbe

Danielle brushed her sleeve across her eyes, catching escaping tears. Lifting the velvet pouch, she reached inside and pulled out the charm. It was a silver clown with a gold teardrop on his cheek. She slipped it around her neck and fastened the clasp.

At one time, it had rested on her mother's chest.

Chills shook her body, and she raised her head to look around her. Slowly, reality reclaimed her muddled brain. What was she doing? What was she thinking? Langley would wake up and wonder what had happened to her. She had to get back to Branson Creek.

Standing, she brushed the damp dirt from her jeans. She would have to tell Langley about the box and the video. Only her uncle had asked her to keep its contents a secret and Langley would never do that. He would turn it over to the FBI.

Of course, she could always drop the video into the well and say she'd never found it. But she wouldn't. The lies and deadly secrets had gone on for much too long.

She held the video up and read the series of numbers printed on the label.

"I'll take that."

The voice slashed into her thoughts. She whirled around and stared into the barrel of Samuel's pistol.

Samuel stepped closer, the weapon pointed at her head. "I knew if I hung around long enough, you'd lead me to the video. Milton's little ace in the hole. Only he didn't have enough sense to take it to the grave with him. Now hand it over."

Danielle swung her hand back and dangled the video over the open well. "Why should I?"

"Because if you don't, I'll have the pleasure of pulling this trigger and blowing you to kingdom come."

"And if I do give it to you, you'll still kill me."

"So the Cajun princess is smart as well as beautiful. But not nearly as noble as you'd have the Randolphs believe. You were too good to take up with me, but you weren't too good to sleep with the cowboy, were you?"

"Thank God, I never went with you."

"No, but you couldn't wait to get your clutches into Langley and the Randolph family money. Going after what you want any way you can. That's a family trait. You got it honest."

"And who did you get your murderous traits from, Samuel? That's what's on the video, isn't it? Evidence that ties you to a murder?"

"Probably more than one. It's just too bad I don't have a camcorder with me right now. You'd make a great movie yourself, screaming as I drop you down that well."

Her blood ran cold. He would do it, she knew. Drop her into a watery grave. Unless she found some way to stop him or to stall him until Langley realized she was missing and came looking for her. Only he'd never think to come here. He'd go back to the cabin.

Samuel's eyes glazed over. His voice was hard, his words clipped. "If you had just died in New Orleans the way you were supposed to, I wouldn't have had to follow you around for the past three weeks, dodging that lame excuse for a lawman and pretending to be your fiancé."

"But why did you try to kill me? I didn't have the video."

"I didn't know that. I thought Milton might have mailed it to you. The attack would have been seen as a simple mugging gone bad. You would have been dead. I would have had the video."

"How did you even know I existed? No one else around here did."

"I saw his letter from you when I came here looking for the evidence Milton had held over my head for the past ten years. He woke up and told me the video was hidden so well I would never find it. He was in pain. I helped him out of it."

Her stomach turned inside out. "You killed a dying man?"

"I admit it wasn't much of a challenge. I just held him down on the bed with a pillow over his face. It wasn't the same rush I'm getting right now watching you sweat."

Still holding the pistol with his right hand, he reached out and grabbed her with his left. His fingers dug into the flesh of her forearm as he yanked her away from the well and closer to him. He put his mouth to her ear.

"I'm twice as good as any cowboy, Danielle. If you want, I could prove it to you before I drop you into the pit."

Her insides shook. Her skin crawled. "Just shoot me, Samuel, and get it over with."

"And miss all the fun?"

She threw the video at the well, but it missed the opening, bouncing off into the grass. Samuel slammed the palm of his hand across her cheek.

"You're really anxious for that cold, lasting swim, aren't you? Imagine what it will be like. You'll try to keep your head above water, but you'll get so tired. And even if the water isn't over your head, you'll lie there in the dark. Wet. Cold. Hungry."

Samuel shoved her hard and she stumbled toward the well. Before she could steady herself, he'd holstered his pistol and grabbed both her arms, twisting them behind her back. She tried to break away, but every time she moved, the pain shot up her arms. If they weren't broken already, they would be any minute.

"You should never have gotten mixed up with your uncle, Danielle. He was evil, and once you did a hit for him, he owned you. Forever."

"Milton's dead, Samuel. He can't rule you anymore. Just take the video and you can walk away."

"Sorry, sweetheart. That might have worked if you'd believed me when I said we were lovers. Now I know how fast you'd go running to Branson Randolph and that brother of his you're so hot for."

He pushed her toward the well. She planted her feet and tried to resist, but he let go his grip just long enough to slam a fist against the side of her head. For a second, the world went dark. When she could see again, she was staring into the black depths of the well.

She didn't want to die. Most of all, she didn't want to die all alone in the watery grave Samuel had planned for her. But her chances for rescue were running out.

She twisted her head to meet his gaze, the hard, angry eyes she'd seen in all her nightmares. He had no conscience and he was going to kill her in cold blood. Without guilt. Without remorse of any kind. The same way her uncle had killed.

He shoved her again. Her right foot slipped over the edge. She was balanced precariously, her only hold on life the hands that twisted her arms mercilessly. He let her down until her feet dangled inside the well. There was nothing under her now but the bottomless pit that waited for her.

She closed her eyes. The grip of amnesia was weakening. The memories of twenty-seven years began to trickle through her mind, but the only face she saw was Langley's.

"Goodbye, Danielle. If you run into Milton, give him my best."

"Go to hell, Drummer."

She felt herself slipping. She kicked wildly, trying to dig her boots into the dirt, but the earth crumbled and crashed into the water below her.

The madman had finally won.

Chapter Fifteen

Langley stepped from the brush, his finger wrapped tightly around the cold metal of the trigger of his .45. One minute, he had caught sight of Danielle being dangled over the well. The next, she had disappeared. Now it was pure ice water that coursed through his veins.

"Drop the pistol, Drummer. Drop it *now*."

"I'm not dropping anything." Samuel leaned over the well and pointed the gun straight into it. "You shoot me, and I'll shoot Danielle. Fair trade, cowboy?"

"Are you all right, Danielle?" He waited for her answer.

"Kill him, Langley. If you don't, he'll kill the both of us. He has the video now, the one he was after."

Langley itched to pull the trigger, but if he did, Samuel would fire into the well. Danielle was a sitting duck. If he didn't shoot Samuel, then the man would do just as Danielle said. He'd kill them both.

His only chance was to distract Samuel, and fast. "Is that what you were looking for, Drummer, the video?"

Samuel kept his gaze on Langley, his gun still pointing into the well. "It's my starring role, compliments of my mentor."

"I'm sure the FBI will be real interested in that. The big boys are coming for you, Drummer."

"They don't know anything about me."

"They know *everything* about you. All they need is the video and they'll lock you away for so long you'll forget the sun is hot."

"But they're never going to get that video."

Langley took a step toward the well. The video lay only a few inches from the edge. And just beyond it, he could see Danielle's fingers, still clutching the rim of the well. Her knuckles were white. She couldn't hold on much longer. He had to act now.

He touched the toe of his right boot to the video. "I'll tell you what. I called my brothers when I couldn't find Danielle. They're on their way over in the helicopter. They should be here any second, so I'll just kick this into the well for safekeeping."

"Get your foot off that video. I'm warning you, Langley."

But Langley was playing the only card he had. "Now that I think about it, they probably won't lock you away for all that long, Samuel. A multiple killer like yourself will probably get the death penalty."

"Don't mess with that video." Sweat beaded on Samuel's brow and rolled down his face.

"You see what it feels like when you're looking death in the eye. It's not as much fun from that end, is it?" Langley kicked the video but not toward the well as he'd threatened. He sent it flying through the air in the opposite direction.

Samuel took the bait. He fired repeatedly, and the video case exploded in a rain of shredded plastic and slivers of tape.

Langley fired, as well, hitting his target dead on. The pistol flew from Samuel's grasp. Yelling profanities, Samuel grabbed his bullet-torn hand and took off into the brush like a scared rabbit. Langley rushed to the well.

He grabbed Danielle's hands and pulled her up. Out of the well and into his arms. She fell against him, talking a mile a minute, but he couldn't hear a word she said over the deafening roar of the helicopter that circled over their heads.

So he just shut her up the best way he knew how, with his mouth on hers.

DANIELLE STOOD AT the front door of the cabin, tired but happy as she waved goodbye to Langley, Mary, Ryder and baby Betsy. She'd thrown a party to celebrate the return of her memory and her life. The entire Randolph family had come and bragged endlessly about her Cajun feast—gumbo, jambalaya and even crawfish étouffée.

It would have been the perfect time for a marriage proposal. She'd even worn the red dress Langley liked so much, only tonight he'd seemed to have no trouble keeping his hands off her.

She walked back inside the cabin, remembering what it had looked like when she'd stepped inside it for the first time. Then she'd shuddered in horror. Now she hated the thought of leaving.

But tomorrow morning, she'd be meeting with Joshua Kincaid. Just as Langley had thought, Wade had sold some of the steers. But Joshua insisted that Wade hadn't pocketed the money. Joshua was bringing a check tomorrow for the full amount received at auction. And he still wanted to purchase the ranch.

She hadn't given him an answer.

The screen door squeaked open behind her. She spun around as Langley stepped inside. "I thought you'd gone home with the others."

"I wanted to make sure you didn't need any more cleanup help."

"It's almost done. I just have a couple of pans left to wash."

Langley stepped to the kitchen door. "It looks like more than a couple to me. Tell you what. I'll wash and you dry." Not waiting for an answer, he picked up a pot and buried it under the suds. "The party was a success," he said, applying a generous helping of elbow grease. "You wowed everyone with your Cajun charm and cooking."

"Did I wow you?"

"Yeah, but I'm easy."

"That's not what Samuel Drummer thinks."

"No, but he's talking now, blabbing everything and hoping for leniency. He admitted he found a letter that you'd written to Milton. You'd included your travel plans and suggested that your uncle keep the video until you got here rather than mailing it as he'd suggested."

"Then why did Samuel think I would have it with me in New Orleans?"

"Because he searched the cabin after he killed your uncle. It wasn't there. He thought your letter might have arrived after he'd mailed the video. And, if all else failed, Samuel had your address in Paris."

"Paris." She stopped drying. "It seems a world away from Kelman, Texas, but it explains why no one reported me as missing. I'd been living there for two years. But my roommate was starting to get worried that I hadn't called. We talked for an hour today. I hate to see my phone bill.''

''At least now you have money to pay it. Not only do you have access to your own funds since you have your identity back, but the ranch is officially yours to sell.''

''But I still don't understand why the hotel I was staying in hadn't noticed that I didn't check out.''

''But you did. Samuel used the hotel key from your purse to go into your room and check you out by video.'' Langley finished rinsing the last pot and set it in the drainer. ''The man's a professional. That's why we didn't find his prints in the house or any of his hairs on the clothes he'd tied around the dummy. It's also why he knew to make up a name and identity for you that couldn't be checked. Your uncle apparently trained him well.''

Danielle stretched and rubbed the muscles in the back of her neck. ''I guess if you've lived your life outside the law like Milton did, it isn't all that surprising that you'd surround yourself with the same kind of people.'' Danielle touched her fingers to the silver charm at her neck. ''But even Milton had a soft spot in his heart for my mother.''

''It would have been far better for you if he hadn't. His soft spot almost got you killed.''

''Ironic, since I came here hoping to find a long-lost uncle and to get my life back.''

Langley dried his hands and stepped away from the sink. ''You were half-successful. The amnesia's lifted. You remember growing up in a small southern Louisiana town with a mother who loved you. And even though she's dead, you have wonderful memories of her.''

''A much nicer heritage than being raised by someone

like Milton. That would have been a bitter pill to swallow.''

He leaned against the counter, finally letting his gaze meet hers. "You've been through a lot, but you'll be able to put the bad behind you when you return to Paris. You're that kind of woman."

"It's not the bad that's troubling me." She took off her apron and laid it across the back of one of the kitchen chairs. "Let's sit on the porch, Langley."

"It's late and it's turned cool."

"Not too cool for me," she teased. "I'm a Cajun woman, remember? We're pretty hot-blooded."

"That's not something I'll likely forget."

He grabbed his Stetson and followed her out the door, but he didn't take the seat beside her in the swing. Instead, he settled on the top step. Close enough to talk. Far enough away their shoulders or thighs wouldn't accidentally brush against each other.

He'd been acting that way ever since she told him that she'd talked to her old boss in Paris and that he'd offered a promotion and a raise when she returned to the consulting firm where she was employed. It seemed as if Langley was resigned to her leaving. But she'd seen his face when he pulled her from the well, and she knew love when she saw it.

"Ryder was cute with Betsy tonight," she said, baiting Langley with talk of babies and family. "He's really getting into the role of daddy."

"I'll say. The way he struts around, you'd think he was the only man to ever get a woman pregnant. And I'm sure you've noticed that my mom misses no opportunity to point out that she knew Betsy was a Randolph all along."

"Come sit by me, Langley." She reached out her hand and beckoned him over. "I'm tired of talking about everyone else. Let's talk about us."

He fingered the brim of his hat, a sure sign she was making him nervous, but he stood and walked over to the swing. She tugged him down beside her.

"I've been thinking about ranching."

"You're meeting with Kincaid tomorrow to discuss his buying the ranch."

"I'm meeting with him, but I've still been thinking about ranching."

"You're a consultant, not a rancher."

She snaked her arm around his shoulders and nibbled on his earlobe. "If I had the right teacher, I could probably learn to be a rancher."

"It might be hard to find a good teacher in Paris."

"I know, but I heard somewhere that if there was anything Langley Randolph didn't know about cows, it probably hasn't been discovered yet."

"You can't believe everything you hear."

"Kiss me, Langley. If you don't want to teach me about cows, then maybe I can teach you a thing or two."

He hesitated. She didn't. She climbed onto his lap and locked her lips with his. The kiss was long and sweet and so rife with passion she was trembling when she came up for air.

"I love you, Langley."

"Why are you doing this, Danielle? Is this some kind of French torture routine I haven't heard of? Leave the man in misery and go flying back to your glamorous life in Paris?"

"The proper response is, I love you, too, Danielle."

He swallowed hard. "I do, you know. I love you more

than I ever dreamed I'd love a woman. But I belong to the ranch as much as it belongs to me. I could never fit in anywhere else."

"I don't have to live in Paris."

He shook his head. "Even if you were willing to stay here with me, I love you way too much to saddle you with a life on the ranch. The novelty would wear off, and you'd miss the excitement of big-city life. You said yourself that you loved it in Paris."

"I did. And now I love it here."

"But you wouldn't be happy here forever, and I couldn't bear to take you for my wife and then have to give you up." He trailed a finger down her cheek and looked into her eyes. "I have nothing to offer you, Danielle, except life on a dusty ranch."

"There are picnics at Branson Creek." She unbuttoned the top buttons of his shirt and tangled her fingers in the hairs on his chest. "There are long, slow kisses and waking up in the morning in your arms. There's you, Langley."

"It would never be enough."

"This isn't the way I planned it, but it looks like it'll have to be the way it is." She dropped to her knees in front of the swing and took his hands in hers. "Marry me, cowboy. I'll even throw in a dowry of a small ranch if you'll say yes quickly."

"Oh, Danielle. You're making this so hard. Not that it wasn't already."

"Believe me, this is much harder on me. My knees are too scratched up to stay on them much longer."

He stood and lifted her in his arms. "You're crazy, do you know that?"

"I've heard rumors."

He kissed her so thoroughly she doubted she could stand alone. Fortunately, she didn't have to. He carried her back inside.

"There's no mattress," he whispered, "but there's a quilt in the bedroom."

"Should I take that as a yes?"

"Are there cows in Texas?"

It took her about two seconds to forget Paris. South Texas with Langley Randolph was as good as it got.

Joanna Wayne is just getting started!

Don't miss the conclusion
of Randolph Family Ties IN557

A MOTHER'S SECRETS

Available wherever Harlequin Intrigue
books are sold!

Chapter One

Kathi Sable opened the front door of her small rented house and scanned the area before stepping onto the porch. Her precaution was more than habit. It was one of the many rules she'd drummed into her brain until they'd become entrenched into her daily routine.

A rule of survival, the same way her frequent moves and name changes were. In this town, she was Susan Campbell, a redhead from Williamsburg, Virginia, who'd moved to Mobile, Alabama, to find work. She handled the office duties for a small construction firm. The boss was great. He asked few questions and didn't give a ding about her past or her private life. He was far too busy trying to keep his wife and his girlfriend happy.

A beige Ford sedan turned the corner and drove slowly down her street. She stepped back inside the door until it passed, but filed the color and type of car away in her mind. She couldn't be too careful.

When the coast was clear, she hurried down the steps and bent to pick up her morning paper. The garage door across the street hummed open and Mr. Scrivener backed down his driveway in his gray minivan. She waved and smiled, playing the part of the nice single neighbor who lived alone and didn't bother anyone.

The role wasn't all that difficult. After all, she'd had almost two years practice and with lots of different neighbors. The names changed. Everything else stayed the same.

Only she liked this street and this house and she loved Mobile. It had a slow, Southern pulse to it, a rhythm that eased some of the pressure she'd come to expect from just being alive. The people were nice, too. She could have made friends easily if she'd been free to do so. But she spent her time alone.

Always alone. It was the ties to other people that tripped you up, made you vulnerable.

Stepping back inside the confines of her cozy house, she made her way down the hall and into the kitchen. The aroma of freshly brewed coffee wafted through the air, and she breathed deeply, drinking it in. Stepping to the counter, she poured her first cup while she glanced at the morning headlines.

A local politician convicted of fraud. Floods in the low-lying areas of the city. A major pileup that claimed five lives in Georgia.

She took a sip of the coffee and then walked to the table so she had enough room to spread out her paper. The inside articles were her favorite. Occasionally, there was something about her home state of Texas, the closest thing she ever got to a letter from home.

She scanned the pages, pausing to read an article on day-care centers and one on a boy who'd saved his friend from drowning in a freak boating accident. And then her eyes slid to the bottom corner.

Ryder Randolph, the youngest brother of Senator Dillon Randolph, was arrested at his home in Kelman, Texas, for questioning about the murder of his one-time friend, Shawn Priest.

The breath rushed from her lungs. She tried to sip the coffee, but her hands trembled so much that the hot liquid spilled over the rim of the mug and slid onto her fingers. She was only distantly aware of the burn.

Kathi finished the article and then read it one more time before pushing the newspaper aside. She'd never thought it would come to this. But it had.

She walked to the window and peered out into the side yard. Her tulips were in full bloom, brilliant blossoms that brushed away the weariness of winter. The dogwood tree in the corner of her backyard was white with tiny cross-shaped blossoms that promised life was starting again.

Only the promises were lies. It was danger that was starting again. Danger and heartbreak, and a past that would never let go. Only she had to make it let go. If not for herself, then for Ryder and for their daughter.

Betsy. Her Betsy. Suddenly, her arms ached with a pain so intense she could barely stand the weight of them.

Her bare feet padded across the cool kitchen floor as she hurried to her bedroom to pack. She had no choice but to step out of the shadows, even if it meant facing a killer.

Shh!

HARLEQUIN®

INTRIGUE®

has a secret…

It's *confidential!*

September 2000

HARLEQUIN®

INTRIGUE®

is proud to present a new trilogy by
JOANNA WAYNE

Branson, Langley and Ryder:
**Randolph brothers, family men,
larger-than-life Texans. Flesh and blood
bind them to each other—and to a
mystery baby girl. One is her father...
all are her protectors.**

#569 THE SECOND SON
June 2000

#573 THE STRANGER NEXT DOOR
July 2000

#577 A MOTHER'S SECRETS
August 2000

Available at your favorite retail outlet.

HARLEQUIN®
Makes any time special ™

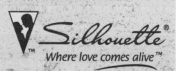

COMING NEXT MONTH

#577 A MOTHER'S SECRETS by Joanna Wayne
Randolph Family Ties

Kathi Sable was in danger. The threat of harm to loved ones had caused her to flee...not realizing she carried Ryder Randolph's child. Now, almost two years later, the forces that sent her on the run drew Kathi back to Ryder's side. Determined to reveal the truth, she needed Ryder's help to end the threat—and make their family reunion last a lifetime.

#578 RENEGADE HEART by Gayle Wilson
More Men of Mystery

Ex-government agent Drew Evans was being hunted for a crime he hadn't committed. The man who could clear Drew's name was dead, leaving his wife and daughter to take up Drew's cause. Though Drew didn't want to involve Maggie Cannon or her daughter, his life depended on questions only she could answer. But once involved, would Drew be able to let Maggie walk away? And would she want to?

#579 INADMISSABLE PASSION by Ann Voss Peterson

Five years ago, secrets shattered Brittany Gerritsen's engagement to Jackson Alcott. Now, opposing attorneys on a high-profile murder case, their exchanges heated up the courtroom—and ultimately blazed in the bedroom. Though a murderer threatened their lives, this time love just might be enough to keep them together.

#580 LITTLE BOY LOST by Adrianne Lee
Secret Identity

When someone stole her identity and her son, Carleen Ellison immediately turned to Kane Kincaid. Though she'd never told him, the child they were searching for was his and the love they'd once shared still burned in her soul. To save his boy and reclaim Carleen's love, Kane would do anything...even if it meant risking his life.

Visit us at www.eHarlequin.com